James Berry grew up to the sound of the Anancy stories as they were told "out in moonlight or in dim paraffin lamplight, during rain and storm winds through empty-belly times or big bellyfuls" in his native village in Jamaica – a country where an oral tradition still thrives.

On coming to England, he was surprised and concerned by how little existing material about the Caribbean there was in schools. His first book, *Bluefoot Traveller*, was an anthology of Anglo-Caribbean poetry for teenagers and he has since compiled several collections of black poets' work. He has also written a number of volumes of verse – including *Fractured Circles* and *Chain of Days* – and was awarded the National Poetry Prize in 1981 for his poem, *Fantasy of an African Boy*. In 1987 his celebrated collection of stories about childhood in the Caribbean – *A Thief in the Village* – won the Smarties Grand Prix award. His book of poems for teenagers, *When I Dance*, received the 1989 Signal Poetry Award.

James Berry has a special interest in multicultural education and gives workshops and readings in schools all over the country. He lives in Sussex.

First published 1988 by Walker Books Ltd
87 Vauxhall Walk, London SE11 5HJ

Text © 1988 James Berry
Illustrations © 1988 Joseph Olubo

This edition published 1989

Printed in Great Britain by Cox and Wyman Ltd, Reading
Typeset by Graphicraft Typesetters Ltd, Hong Kong

British Library Cataloguing in Publication Data
Berry, James 1924-
Anancy-Spiderman.
I. Title II. Olubo, Joseph
823' 914[J]   PZ7
ISBN 0-7445-1311-1

ANANCY-SPIDERMAN

WRITTEN BY
JAMES BERRY

ILLUSTRATED BY
JOSEPH OLUBO

WALKER BOOKS
LONDON

FOREWORD

I want to thank Mother Africa for this wonderful character of Anancy and for these stories and all the others Anancy inspired. I want to thank my ancestors who travelled with the stories and transplanted them in the Caribbean. I want to thank my parents for keeping their links with the stories and for passing them on to us in our Jamaican village, out in moonlight or in dim paraffin lamplight, during rain and storm winds, through empty-belly times or big bellyfuls. I want to thank our folklorist Louise Bennett for writing and publishing her telling of Anancy stories. I want to thank Walter Jekyll for his resourceful collecting of these stories, preserving their authenticity and providing a big body of a printed record in his book *Jamaica Song and Story*. I want to thank friends in England who have read my telling of Anancy and given their helpful suggestions. I want to thank the publishers for providing me with the pleasurable opportunity of writing *Anancy-Spiderman*.

* * *

Anancy, the spider hero of Westindian folk tales, originated in Ghana as the Ashanti Spider God. Sly and soft and sweet voiced, he can be anything from a lovable rogue to an artful prince. Often, he gets overwhelmed by a terrible greed he cannot help. Essentially both spider and man, his nature allows him to change as the situation demands. This ability to change himself, and leave the ground, vanish into a tree or into the housetop to hide, makes him godlike. That is also linked with the way he causes good and bad things to come into the world for the first time, continue to happen and become part of life.

On the face of it Anancy has nothing to use to counter the superiority of an opponent. You see, he relies on his wits and his cunning. His usual opponent is the mighty Tiger. Against that massive size, that destruction-capacity, little weaponless Anancy has to win, and survive, without physical combat. His opponents fall for his oiled and honeyed tongue – just like the way his audience sides with him – because, with his guileless approach, his innocent presence, his cunning is never suspected. Yet, Anancy doesn't at all always manage to impose his will and way.

Certainly, Anancy gets his revenge on Tiger at the dance contest at the "John-Canoo and the Shine-Dancer-Shine Event". But at the "Stump-a-Foot Celebration Dance" Tiger plays the game the wrong way and undermines Anancy's advantages and spoils his possible glory. Similarly, in "Anancy and Storm and the Reverend Man-Cow", Anancy's friends have to save him from the plot he cooked up which would lead to his own public disgrace. Also, in "Mrs Anancy, Chicken Soup and Anancy", Mrs Anancy deprives him of one of his big-feast moments and turns the eating into a charitable village act.

Some of the stories in this book are stories we had told to us as children and which we learnt from other village sources and told back to each other. I have expanded all of these. Other stories I have developed from traditional versions and themes. In an overall way, I have deepened, clarified and expanded the stories. I have brought in those parts of the stories usually left out in oral tellings. The ways of characters, their situations, motives, hopes, beliefs, were already known, well shared and well understood, by both audience and storyteller. Those parts were not brought out openly at all in a telling. It seemed to me that in cold print much of that left-out information was needed.

Right from the start I decided I would not keep Anancy confined within a restricted characterisation and narrative, which he had obviously outgrown. His inventive resourcefulness, his vocal zest and cunning, his outlandish ideas and ways all called out for an expanded staging. So Anancy here is the African Anancy showing his new Caribbean roots. He appears as the Caribbean mythological figure and symbol he has developed into. Familiar Caribbean characters with him – like Dog, Puss, Goat, Jackass – all come on to the stage with Anancy.

In spelling the name as it is – Anancy – I have kept the old Jamaican spelling instead of using the more recently appeared "Anansi" – the African way. My reason for this is emotional, aesthetic and cultural. In his new world the folk-hero character has taken on much that is new. For me, this familiar spelling has roots magic, a sense of originality, and an association with oral truth.

JAMES BERRY
June 1987

CONTENTS

For
Sista-Maud,
Cousn-Oley, Brodda-Hervan,
Sista-Neat, Alfie, Berry,
Ben and Doley

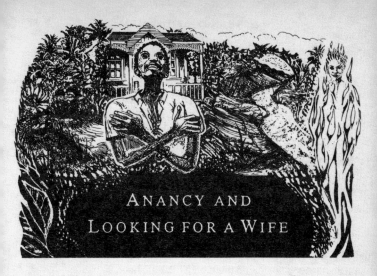

ANANCY AND
LOOKING FOR A WIFE

Anancy finds himself ready to have a wife. He has a lovely place where he lives. Anancy-Spiderman even has a clean stream running through his yard. But from the time wanting-a-wife stings Anancy, he begins to go funny.

Anancy sees Red Flowers together and Anancy gets fooled. Red Flowers are there close together dancing in Wind and Anancy thinks it's a girl. Red Flowers laugh at Anancy and say, "Can't you see we're just flowers and not a girl?"

Another time Anancy sees Rainbow in the sky and begs Rainbow to come down and become his bride. Anancy is there staring at Rainbow when Rainbow disappears.

Anancy goes walking through a green pasture. Everything is wonderful to Anancy. Sunlight is like gold surrounding him. Wind is the magic of a most fantastic wife who'll be beside him one day.

Anancy comes under a big spreading fig tree, where everybody usually stops and rests. But now, nobody is about anywhere. As if somebody whispers in his ear, Anancy stops. He looks round. Crickets and birds make noise in bright midday sun-heat.

Anancy sees a shining shape flickering, under low branches of the tree. The shape is like a big and strange bird preening itself. But the shape is also like a slender plant with blooms glowing. Then the shape is all a golden light flickering.

There is the crackle of a gentle fire burning. Anancy goes closer.

The fire is a pretty flame burning in the shade. As he sees the flame closer, a kind of magic works on Anancy. Bewitched, the Anancy-Spiderman steps up even closer yet.

Anancy sees. Anancy feels. Anancy understands now that the flame is a pretty-pretty girl all alone.

Anancy stares. He is lost to everything else. Anancy just walks round and round the pretty flame.

"Hello," Anancy says.

"Hello," Flame answers back, quietly.

Anancy is happy. Anancy is too-too impressed and excited. Such a big mark is made on him, Anancy can't talk. He bursts out singing:

"O, O! Palm trees have open arms.
O, O! Fire's a loving storm.
Rainbow – stay up high and far,
Red bloom is a red-red star.
Flame walks with me
Rain dries up round me, O.
Flame walks with me
Rain dries up round me, O.
  Dries up round me, O.
    Dries up round me, O!"

Anancy stops singing. He says, "Miss Flame. Oh, Miss Flame. Will you give Bro Nancy a visit tomorrow?"

With a gentle crackle in her voice, Flame answers in her quiet way, "I will come. I will come and visit Bro Nancy tomorrow." And now, Flame carries on talking.

Flame asks Anancy to be on his own when she arrives to see him.

"I'll travel on my own," Flame says.

But most important, Flame points out that for her to walk to his house, Anancy will have to prepare a trail. He'll have to put down a trail of dry sticks and twigs and dry leaves and dry grass. The trail should be laid through the woods, on through the gate of the pasture, on through the village, through his gateway and right on to the door of his house.

Next day, Anancy rises early. Quick and brisk, Anancy gathers up all the dry sticks, dry twigs, dry leaves and dry grass. And Anancy fixes the trail for Miss Flame to follow, all perfect-perfect.

Happy and excited, Anancy begins to sing and dance. Over and over Anancy sings this little song:

> "Today! Today! It's to be.
> Today! Today! It's to be.
> Miss Flame – Miss Flame – a-visit me.
> Miss Flame – Miss Flame – a-visit me.
> I roll round and round and round the moon.
> I roll round and round and round the moon.
> Miss Flame is here soon-soon.
> Miss Flame is here soon-soon, O!"

All the time Anancy is singing, Flame is coming along steady-steady. And mischievous Wind runs and runs in and out of Flame to help Flame. But mostly, Wind keeps arms around Flame, pressing, helping Flame along.

All golden and beautiful, Flame's feet go on eating up the trail of dry sticks, twigs, leaves and grass. Flame comes steady-steady through the woods, through the pasture, through the village. Yet nobody sees Flame travelling.

Then, Anancy sees Flame coming down the road. Flame smokes and waves about in Wind. Anancy speeds up his dancing. And he sings louder:

> *"Today! Today! It's to be.*
> *Today! Today! It's to be.*
> *Miss Flame – Miss Flame – a-visit me.*
> *Miss Flame – Miss Flame – a-visit me.*
> *I roll round and round and round the moon.*
> *I roll round and round and round the moon.*
> *Miss Flame is here soon-soon.*
> *Miss Flame is here soon-soon, 0!"*

Flame turns into Anancy's yard-gate making the most awful whip-cracking noises. One look now and Anancy-Spiderman is worse than frightened. His face is terror itself. Flame is no longer little and beautiful. Flame is now a big and roaring and terrible Blazing-Fire.

Red-hot, Blazing-Fire is huge, fifty times bigger than little Flame. And Wind works with Blazing-Fire. Wind works whipping up Blazing-Fire, making Blazing-Fire increase in leaps and spread. And Blazing-Fire smokes bad-bad like a great pile of burning and moves quick-quick towards Anancy's doorway.

Anancy stands with arms spread wide, as if he can stop Blazing-Fire. He waves his arms about and shouts, "Go back! Go back! I change my mind about you. Go back. Go back, I say. I change my mind." Anancy has to jump back, to get himself away from the quick moving heat.

Oh, Bro Nancy works like six crazy men to save his house!

Fast-fast, Bro Nancy sweeps the trail of dry sticks, dry twigs, dry leaves and dry grass, away from his house. Bro Nancy shoves the trail away from his doorway, sweeping it over to the stream running through his yard. And all this time, oh, Blazing-Fire shoots out tongues of flames and sparks and smoke to cripple Anancy, but misses.

Not at all able to stop itself, Blazing-Fire is taken by the trail right over the edge of the stream.

Blazing-Fire falls straight into the pool of the stream. Oh, Anancy manages such a narrow escape!

Yet the dying Blazing-Fire spits out and splutters, keeping crying out. But Blazing-Fire goes smaller and smaller, drowning.

The Blazing-Fire becomes only a smell of burning. Blazing-Fire disappears. It goes completely. It could no more be seen.

From that day, water is used to stop fire. Anancy-Spiderman has a hand in it. All the same, Anancy doesn't stop. Anancy goes on looking for a wife.

ANANCY, OLD WITCH
AND KING-DAUGHTER

From the day King-Daughter is born, King-Wife decides she'll keep her girl child's name a secret. King-Wife sees that if her daughter's name isn't known, guessing it will be a test for the man who wants to marry her when she grows up. King-Wife smiles to herself saying, "Yes. That will be good. That will make him show how clever he really is. The first one – the first one who guesses her name – shall marry my daughter."

All servants at the palace become well warned. "Tell no one Daughter's name."

Every servant swears on oath. "Never ever will I let Daughter's real name come from my lips to anyone outside this big and beautiful palace."

King-Daughter is to be talked about only as "Daughter".

Then one day everybody begins to talk. "King-Daughter is old enough to marry." "What?" "Yes, yes, yes! King-Daughter is old enough to marry."

From everywhere, rich and famous young men begin to go in their carriages to the palace, to guess King-Daughter's name.

When Anancy hears what is happening, Anancy becomes excited. Anancy walks up and down saying to himself, "Bro Nancy, you have a chance. You know you have a good-good chance to marry King-Daughter."

Anancy goes to see Bro Dog.

"Bro Dog," Anancy says, "suppose – just suppose – you and me should play a game, could you be a first-class partner?"

"Bro Nancy," Dog says, "you know very well I'm never second class. Whatever I agree to I agree to."

"Well," Anancy says, "how smart a bad man beggar can you be?"

"A bad man and a beggar together?"

"I think I'm thinking like that," Anancy says.

"I can try," Dog says. "I can try."

Anancy dresses Dog. Anancy works on Dog till Dog looks like a scabby, ragged, dirty and smelly beggar.

"Bro Dog," Anancy says, "oh, you look perfect."

"Perfect what?" Dog says.

"Perfectly awful. Perfect bad man beggar to be scorned, hated, despised."

"What?" Dog says. "Suppose I get hurt?"

"Bro Dog, all the time, we'll be together," Anancy assures him.

Dog and Anancy take a short cut and come to a famous royal picnic spot. They both hide themselves behind bushes.

7

Palace servants arrive ahead by themselves. They spread cloths and mats on the grass, put out picnic baskets together and sit awaiting the royal party.

Bro Dog creeps up behind the backs of the servants. He snatches the prettiest cloth, with DAUGHTER embroidered on it, and begins running about with it. Furious, the servants leap up and rush at Bro Dog.

"Drop it," they demand. "Nasty old mangy dog, drop it. Drop the cloth!" Dog rushes about playfully and then attempts to run away with the cloth. A royal maid runs after Dog. Really wild, she shouts, "Mangy dog, drop Princess Basamwe's picnic cloth!"

Dog immediately drops the cloth and runs away.

All the way home, Anancy sings:

> *"Nobody knows her name.*
> *Nobody knows her name.*
> *Then who is Princess Basamwe?*
> *Who is Princess Basamwe, O?*
> *Princess Basamwe, Basamwe, Basamwe."*

Anancy becomes determined not to make any mistakes. It seems most important to Anancy that he should go and see Old Witch. But Old Witch needs money. Where can he get money?

Anancy remembers where money is. He goes and steals a gold piece from Bro Monkey. What Anancy doesn't know is that Monkey keeps the pile of gold pieces in the cave for Old Witch.

Anancy goes to see Old Witch in her plain earth-floor thatch-house. Old Witch sits surrounded by Snake, Alligator and a long leg Jumby Bird. Old Witch doesn't ask Anancy to sit, only to put down his piece of gold. Old Witch notices the gold but doesn't say she knows it comes from her own pile of gold pieces.

Old Witch works her tricks with Anancy. She tells him a certain time when he should start out for the palace. She tells him he'll find himself suited out with everything, at that certain time.

At that certain time next day Anancy can't believe his good luck. He suddenly finds himself dressed like a prince – perfect-perfect. He steps out of his door. And there a horse and carriage awaits him.

Carrying gifts, Anancy arrives at the palace in his shining open-top carriage. Anancy looks everything of a best-dressed prince. He stands proud-proud in his carriage at the palace gate and begins to sing:

"Nobody knows her name.
Nobody knows her name.
Then who is Princess Basamwe?"

As Anancy calls the name Basamwe the palace gate swings open wide. Anancy's carriage drives up to the palace door. He stands in his carriage and sings:

"Nobody knows her name.
Nobody knows her name.
Then who is Princess Basamwe?
Who is Princess Basamwe, O?
Princess Basamwe, Basamwe, Basamwe."

The King, King-Wife, King-Daughter and the whole royal family come out on the big veranda. As the stare of

King-Daughter's eyes touches Anancy, his horse and carriage vanishes. King-Daughter blinks; Anancy's top hat vanishes. She blinks again; his shoes vanish. She blinks again; his jacket, then his watch and chain, his walking stick, his trousers, all vanish. As he's going to be naked he finds himself standing in his own ordinary clothes, clutching his gifts of silver sandals, necklace and headdress. Anancy turns into spider and disappears.

Anancy hurries back to Old Witch.

Hurrying along, in his ordinary clothes again – without princely carriage, without princely dress – Anancy says to himself, "Oh well, nice things come, nice things go. Even day comes, day goes, like magic." But Anancy knows that somehow his stolen gold piece given to Old Witch has made her cross. Her angry spell has stripped him. Yet Anancy reminds himself, "Old Witch has done something. She's done something. She'll have to do another something!"

Anancy comes into Old Witch house and again stands on her plain earth-floor. Snake, Alligator and Jumby Bird are there with Old Witch. Before Anancy can open his mouth to speak Old Witch speaks. Not even looking at Anancy, Old Witch says, "Go and hand your gifts to the first three women you meet. Go, as I say."

Anancy leaves. And one after the other, Anancy gives away his gifts to women he meets, as Old Witch says. And, something the least expected happens.

The woman he hands his last-last gift to becomes Anancy's wife.

ANANCY AND THE
MAKING OF THE BRO TITLE

At the time, nobody is called Bro.

Anancy gets everybody to spread news that something special is ready to happen. It's ready to happen because everybody is ready for it. Come to the meeting in the village square. The big new happening will be revealed.

Anancy is pleased-pleased. A big crowd surrounds him in the early night. Anancy feels good and ready to make a sweetmouth speech.

"Friends," he starts, "you know and I know, everybody is a good-good person. But every person uses only a little goodness and a little bigness. People give teeny bits of gifts, a sprinkle of kind words, a pinch of this and a pinch of that. Friends, just think now of all the big extras that can come from making goodness work bigger and better."

"Hear, hear!" somebody says.

"Thank you, Dog," Anancy says.

"Friends," Anancy goes on, "make bigness work, and your fields are always full of harvest, your cupboards are always full of food."

"How can goodness make things happen just like that?" Rabbit asks.

"By becoming a Bro, which means Brother," Anancy says. "He who holds the title of Bro accepts everybody as brother. A Bro is building a little house; a Bro from every house comes and helps the building of a big house. A Bro is planting a little field; a Bro from every house comes and helps the planting of a big field. Drought is on; every Bro becomes rainmaker. It's hurricane; every Bro together clears up disaster. It's eating and drinking and dancing; every Bro and kinfolks are together in big merriment."

"Hear, hear!" Dog says.

"The title of Bro is good, but why no title of Sis for sister?" Anancy's wife says.

"Dear wife, thank you. But 'Bro' stands for 'Sis' as well."

"Dear husband, you well-well know Bro doesn't stand for Sis."

"Yes, dear wife, it stands for Sis, till one day, one day."

"Till one day, one day, what?"

"One day when you get your Sis title."

"Will we work on it together?"

"Yes," Anancy says. "We'll work on it together."

"And this is a good-good promise?"

"Yes, dear wife. This is a good-good promise, because everybody's ready to have their bigness, have their abundantness, their beautifulness, their wonderfulness!"

"Hear, hear!" Dog says.

"Friends," Anancy goes on, "take on the title of Bro in

front of your name and you have a mummah and a puppah in every house. No bad-mouth will hurt you and loved ones. No bad-mind will work on you and loved ones. No bad spell, no curse, no enemy will get you and loved ones. You are to be killed and everybody saves you. You are to be hungry and every family feeds you. You are sick and every family worries about you, gets you balm and heals you. Everybody is brother, everybody is friend. No enemies anywhere."

"Hear, hear!" Dog says. "Hip, hip, hooray!"

"Hip, hip, hooray!" the crowd say. "Hip, hip, hooray! Hip, hip, hooray!"

Anancy breaks into song:

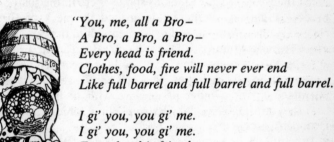

"You, me, all a Bro—
A Bro, a Bro, a Bro—
Every head is friend.
Clothes, food, fire will never ever end
Like full barrel and full barrel and full barrel.

I gi' you, you gi' me.
I gi' you, you gi' me.
Every head is friend.
Clothes, food, fire will never ever end
Like full barrel and full barrel and full barrel.

You, me, all, a Bro—
A Bro, a Bro, a Bro—
Make chain of full baskets,
Make chain of full baskets
Long-long, longer than day,
Long-long, longer than day,
Longer than day, O,
Longer than day, O!"

In noises and cheering, people rush forward. People want to be called Bro. Anancy puts his arm around Monkey. Anancy raises his other arm to the crowd and says, "Friends, I am your Bro Nancy. This is your Bro Monkey!" The crowd cheer them. Anancy gives Bro Monkey a big bag of corn. Rabbit becomes a Bro and gets two good cuts of cedar board from Anancy. Dog becomes a Bro and gets a shining necklace. Nearly everybody comes forward and becomes a Bro.

Next day early-early Anancy is ready to travel into everybody's country to spread the news about becoming a Bro.

In Anancy's yard, Bro Jackass stands there in the shaft of a cart. A garland of flowers is around the neck of Bro Jackass. Others with musical instruments sit in the cart. Bro Monkey has a drum, Bro Dog a banjo, Bro Rabbit a flute and Bro Puss a tambourine. Everybody is decorated with a garland of flowers or leaves. Peacock and Turkey have no instruments. Three other people are without instruments too; they are One-Eye Pig, Broken-Wing John Crow and Dropped-Leg Goat.

Though Jackass knows his way, Bro Nancy sits in the cart in front looking like the driver.

Bro Nancy picks up his sawn-off cowhorn and begins to blow it like a foghorn. That tells everybody something eventful is happening. In the sound of the horn, Anancy and his party start out with music and singing:

> *"You, me, all a Bro—*
> *A Bro, a Bro, a Bro—*
> *Every head is friend . . ."*

With groups of people following them sometimes, Anancy

and his band of people travel till they come into Blackbird country.

Anancy begins to blow his cowhorn at great lengths to arouse the bird-people to the event of his arrival. And he and his band come to a road lined with Blackbird KlingKling-people cheering them and singing and clapping and dancing for them. In the sounds of the cowhorn and their music, they go on to a big square and find Chiefman Blackbird in official colours waiting for them.

As the crowd of Blackbird-people surround them, Anancy and his party play on and on and sing:

"You, me, all a Bro–
A Bro, a Bro, a Bro–
Every head is friend…

As the music and singing end, Bro Turkey says, "Gobble gobble gobble gobble gobble!" Bro Peacock opens out his tail and spins. One-Eye Pig stares bright-bright, smiling. Broken-Wing John Crow and Dropped-Leg Goat flap and hop about in a little dance.

Anancy stands up in the cart and makes his speech about becoming a Bro.

In loud cheering Anancy steps down from his cart and embraces Chiefman Blackbird KlingKling. He declares Chiefman Blackbird and his people all a Bro.

Anancy hands out gifts, gets gifts himself and moves off again blowing his cowhorn, with his band, playing and singing, "You, me, all a Bro."

In the same way as before, Anancy and his party travel on and stop in Yellow-Snake country, in Monkey, Patoo, Rabbit, Hawk, John Crow and Ratbat countries, and then go on to Tiger country.

Here, in Tiger country, Anancy is to find more than usual resistance.

A great crowd of Tiger-people stand around Anancy and his party.

As usual, Bro Monkey bangs his drum, Bro Dog strums his banjo, Bro Rabbit plays his flute, Bro Puss shakes his tambourine. At the end of the music and singing, Bro Turkey says, "Gobble gobble gobble gobble gobble!" Bro Peacock opens out his tail and spins. One-Eye Pig stares bright-bright, smiling. Broken-Wing John Crow and Dropped-Leg Goat flap and hop about in their little dance. The Tiger-people clap and cheer.

Anancy gets going with his sweetmouth speech. The Tiger-people listen and listen keen-keen. Then sudden-sudden Chiefman Tiger stops Anancy, saying, "Anancy, I can defend myself. My people can defend themselves, in a group or as individuals. Why do we need this Bro business? I myself, I don't want to go and sit about with other people one bit. And you talk about getting hungry. We may get hungry, but certainly not for long. You talk about giving and getting. Why should I want to be given anything when I can take as I like?"

"Because as a Bro other Bro people won't be frightened of you," Anancy says.

"But I like other people to be frightened of me," Chiefman Tiger says. "I like people to hide when I walk past. It's great."

"Would it be the same," Anancy says, "if people didn't hide? If different people talked to you? And cheered you openly for your honour and your beauty and you knew that people talked about your good temper and the beautiful gentleman you are? Would it all be the same?"

Chiefman Tiger thinks, then in surprise he says, "Me a

beautiful gentleman? Me having some honour?"

"Yes," Anancy says.

"Nobody has ever said that. How else am I beautiful?"

"Well," Anancy says, "your coat – the coat of all Tiger-people – is a blessing. Your handsome head and strong-strong shoulders are all a blessing. The Bro title comes to you and all Tiger-people as a much later blessing."

"Is this true? Is all this true?"

"It's true. Bro title gives you a new status. With it you become Bro Chiefman Tiger. And once you're a Bro you can go on to become Mister."

"Me become Mister?"

"Yes," Anancy says. "You can even go on from Mister to Sir and on to Honourable."

"What will I become then?" Chiefman Tiger asks.

"You'll be Honourable Sir Mister Bro Chiefman Tiger."

"Wow!" Chiefman Tiger says. "With all the weight of that honour, I couldn't walk. I'd have to be carried."

A great laughter and cheering goes up.

"Tell me how I'll actually get all that honour," Chiefman Tiger says. "How I'll know I've got it. And everybody'll know I've got it. And tell me more about the good things about me I don't know and about all I'll get if I become a Bro."

"Well," Anancy says, "if you treat, say, Bro Monkey or Bro Rabbit or Bro Dog – all other people – like they are your own Tiger-people, the news will come back to me. And I'll see you get your honour in front of everybody."

Chiefman Tiger goes silent, then says, "But I don't want to be good to everybody. I want to be very bad to some people. I have a lot of badness I must use. Can I start being good to some people who aren't Tiger-people and go on being very bad to others?"

"Chiefman, Chiefman Tiger," Anancy says, "to be a Bro means everybody makes their own country a place of Bro, and so, at the same time, everybody makes all the countries one big place of Bro."

"Wow!" Chiefman Tiger says. "All this is new! Very new!"

"Yes," Anancy says. "Very new. But everybody is ready for it."

"I like the honour I'll get," Chiefman Tiger says. "I like the honour very much. But there is a spot of bother, I must admit. You see, as it is now, I can walk through anybody's country, and, apart from Lion, nobody, nobody can stop me. Or even challenge me. I have that safeguard already."

"Yes," Anancy says, "that's really so, Chiefman Tiger. But mightn't you get some news from Monkey-people or Rabbit-people, if when you walk through their country you were able to stop and have a chat, and have some refreshments they give you?"

"Hear, hear!" the Tiger-people say. "Hear, hear!"

Chiefman Tiger goes silent for a little while. Then he looks up and says, "Anancy, I'll join."

"Hear, hear!" the Tiger-people say. "Hear, hear!"

Bro Nancy comes and puts his arms around Chiefman Tiger. The Tiger-people become Bro. Anancy gives the people gifts. In turn, the Tiger-people pile on their gifts in Anancy's cart.

Anancy and his cart-band of people leave Tiger country in an uproar of cheering, cowhorn blowing and music and singing.

At home again, Anancy finds he has come into a new and difficult problem. How should he share out the cartload of gifts? Anancy tells his cart-band of people that silence has overtaken him.

"Silence has come upon me, friends," Anancy tells them.

"It is like a night a man must sleep in. Welcome in different countries make a man happy and sad. Unbrothers have become brothers. It calls for silence and fasting. I must have silence and fasting for seven days and seven nights."

Everybody is struck by Anancy's new mood. All agree to help Bro Nancy and leave him alone. "Let Bro Nancy deal with his deep mind," they say.

Anancy will have nothing to do with the gifts. Anancy lets his cart-band of people unload the cart and carry the bags of rabbits and birds, box of dried fish, barrel of crabs, barrels of different corned meat, bags of corn and dry beans, bags of yams, spices, bottles of rum and baskets of fruit and puddings and bread, and stack them in his kitchen.

The moment Anancy sees that everyone is really gone – and everywhere is quiet-quiet – Anancy leaps up and begins to dance and sing around the pile of gifts:

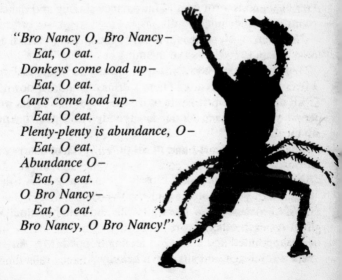

> "Bro Nancy O, Bro Nancy –
>   Eat, O eat.
> Donkeys come load up –
>   Eat, O eat.
> Carts come load up –
>   Eat, O eat.
> Plenty-plenty is abundance, O –
>   Eat, O eat.
> Abundance O –
>   Eat, O eat.
> O Bro Nancy –
>   Eat, O eat.
> Bro Nancy, O Bro Nancy!"

Anancy drinks rum and sings and dances. He begins to season and pickle different meats for keeping. At the same time, he cooks a sample of every kind of the meat and of everything else. And the more the kitchen gets stronger with the smell of cooking and spices and seasoning the more Anancy sips his drink, takes a taste of things and sings and dances.

Almost bursting with food and drink, Anancy falls asleep.

Anancy wakes up in his long furry gown. Anancy sings and dances round the gifts, and drinks, cooks, eats and falls asleep again.

Not caring whether it is day or night, Anancy drinks, dances and sings, cooks and eats and falls asleep for three days.

Worried about her husband, Mrs Anancy arrives at the kitchen doorway. She cannot really believe what she sees. Her husband is a round and fat Anancy singing and dancing round a smaller pile of gifts.

Mrs Anancy steps inside, looks round and is shocked. She asks Anancy, "What's the meaning of all this?"

"Wife," Anancy says, "sit down and join your husband. Lots of meals are ready. There's drink. Come, sit down."

"I'll have none of it. None of it," she says. "The gifts were never yours to have alone. Everybody will have to know about this."

"Shall I promote your title of Sis or not?" Anancy says with a threat.

"Not," Mrs Anancy says crossly. "Promoting a Sis title is bigger than you. Much bigger than you."

"Wife," Anancy says, "you are wife and I am husband. We don't let each other down."

Disappointed and angry but feeling trapped, Mrs Anancy gives a loud sigh and sits down heavily.

Somewhere, loud-loud, unexpectedly, Blackbird Kling-Kling begins to sing this little song:

> *"People, O people,*
> *Come and see Bro Nancy.*
> *People, O people,*
> *Come and see Bro Nancy.*
> *Come and see Bro Nancy, O!*
> *Come and see Bro Nancy, O!..."*

Other Blackbird-people begin to sing this same song, passing the news round the whole village.

Sudden-sudden, the yard is full of people.

Anancy's cart-band of people are the first to arrive. Immediately, Anancy says, "Oh, Bro Dog, Bro Monkey, Bro Jackass, and everybody, so pleased you've come! So, so glad-glad you heard the KlingKling call! Come. We'll put out long tables and benches. We'll put out the cooked meats with everything cooked. We'll cook more meat and everything else. We'll have all the drinks and get some more. We'll strike up the music. And Bro and Bro and Bro and everybody, when the merriment is on, and you see Anancy dancing, know that Anancy dances away his badness. With all his heart, Anancy dances away his badness."

That whole day and night, Anancy's yard becomes a place of great feasting and merriment.

From that time, leaders always try to cover up the lion-share of things they take for themselves.

ANANCY, DOG AND
OLD HIGUE DRY-SKULL

Bro Nancy doesn't go hunting with the hunters that day. It's Bro Dog and others who go hunting. And everybody shoots and catches something, except Dog. Every hunter has a bagful of birds and wild animals. Bro Dog alone turns home with an empty bag. Sad, tired and hungry, Bro Dog decides to hang back from the others and take a short cut home by himself.

Alone, halfway in the woods, Dog stumbles on something like a bone. Bro Dog can't resist a bone. Bro Dog stops, but is disappointed.

"Oh, blow it!" Dog says to himself. "Why couldn't it be a fresh bone with flesh? Why couldn't I have a meal?" Dog can't help looking at the bone better and seeing it's a dry-skull. He decides he'll just leave it, then finds himself thinking, "I'm so hungry. Might as well put it in my bag and have a bit of chew off it later." So Bro Dog picks up the dry-skull and puts it in his empty bag.

As Bro Dog walks on, he notices the bag hanging from his shoulder is getting heavier and heavier.

"Nonsense," Bro Dog says to himself. "How can my bag get heavier? I must be just hungry and weak."

But as Bro Dog walks on, his bag gets so heavy that his shoulder can't take the weight any longer. He has to rest the bag down. And Dog naturally has the urge to look inside the bag to see what's happened. Dog is dumbfounded. Dog can't open his bag. Dog struggles and struggles and no way can he open his own bag. Dog stops trying.

"Blow it!" Dog says to himself. "I'm too hungry and tired to bother with all this. I'll just leave it – the whole lot." Bro Dog takes his hands off the bag, stands up and begins to walk away.

"You can't leave me. You see me you can't leave me," a squeaky voice from the bag says. "Pick me up, Bro Dog. Put me on your back."

Bro Dog knows now he's really in trouble. He knows, he has picked up Old Higue Dry-Skull. Old Higue is the worst thing in the whole world. It holds you in its spell and takes your blood. Old Higue Dry-Skull is equally nasty and horrible and terrible. Dog could have died. All his bad-luck has come one day.

Bro Dog hesitates. But Bro Dog finds himself trying to lift the heavy bag.

"You can pick me up," the squeaky voice says. "You can pick me up. Put me on your back."

Bro Dog somehow manages to lift the bag onto his back and put the straps round his head.

Knowing he dares not stop, knowing too he doesn't know what he'll do with Old Higue Dry-Skull, Bro Dog walks and

walks with his load like a man on his back. Bro Dog comes
out into the village wondering what he'll ever do with his
burden or what it'll ever do with him.

The first person Dog is to see is Bro Anancy. Seeing Dog
under his big load, Anancy's greedy eyes pop. And poor Bro
Nancy can't help himself. He steps brisk-brisk up to Dog.
Listen now to the sweet voice of Bro Nancy. "Oh, a
good-good evening to you, Bro Dog. Seems for certain the
hunt has favoured you with best-best of luck."

"I'm tired, Bro Nancy," Dog says. "Tired-tired! I have
more on my back than I can manage."

"Bro Dog," Anancy says, "you know I'll help you. Let me
help you."

"Oh, Bro Nancy," Dog says, "it's just what I need. I won't
even bother to put it down."

"No, Bro Dog," Anancy says. "Just put your load straight
onto my back."

"Thank you. Oh, thank you, Bro Nancy," Dog says, "for
taking my load. So tired-tired, I'll just sit down right here a
bit."

"That's all right, Bro Dog," Anancy says. "Now it's on my
back, I'll just walk on. I'll take your load to your house. Or
my house."

"Bro Nancy," Dog says, "it doesn't matter. I know where
you live. You know where I live."

Bro Nancy goes off with Old Higue Dry-Skull. Relieved,
Bro Dog merely goes off to his own house. Bro Dog well
knows Anancy will take the heavy bag to his own house
expecting to find a bagful of fresh meat. That is so. But
instead of finding fresh meat Anancy finds trouble.

Bro Nancy opens the bag easy-easy. But Anancy jumps
back. He can't believe his bad luck when he sees Old Higue
Dry-Skull in the bag staring at him.

"You take me, you take me out the bag," the squeaky voice says. "You take me out the bag, Bro Nancy."

Anancy knows he's in the spell of Old Higue Dry-Skull. He knows Old Higue Dry-Skull lives on something alive put beside him every two days to quick-quick shrivel up and wither away. He knows, under his spell, you become his slave and can't go anywhere beyond a certain distance.

Anancy has to take Old Higue Dry-Skull out of the bag. He has to take on looking after him and becoming his constant companion. All the same, Bro Nancy is not a man to put up with anything.

Anancy racks and racks his brains to find a way to free himself of Old Higue Dry-Skull.

One day Anancy hears Chicken-Hawk excite his chickens outside. Anancy runs off from Old Higue Dry-Skull saying he must protect his chickens. Anancy sees Hawk eating one of his chickens on a tree stump. Hawk is about to fly off with the chicken but Anancy waves and gestures and calls in a panic voice. Hawk sees Anancy wants to talk to him badly. Hawk waits and listens.

Anancy tells Hawk he'll give him a whole coop of chickens if he'll do a job for him quickly.

You see, every day after twelve o'clock Anancy has to put Old Higue Dry-Skull outside to sun himself. Also, Anancy knows that open wings overhead drive terror in Old Higue Dry-Skull more than anything else in the world.

Next day, Anancy puts Old Higue Dry-Skull outside in the open and stands back in hiding to watch everything.

Chicken-Hawk comes overhead and begins to circle round. Hawk's shadow moves over Old Higue Dry-Skull and he's thrown into terrible terror.

"Anancy! Anancy!" the squeaky voice calls in panic. "Hawk's overhead. Hawk's overhead! Come and take me in. Take me in, Bro Nancy! You put me here. Come and take me in! Take me in!"

Hawk swoops down with open talons, picks up Old Higue Dry-Skull, flies off on and on and drops him in deepest woods.

To get even with Dog, Anancy takes Hawk and shows him an easy and quiet way into Dog's chicken coop. For seven days Hawk comes and carries off one of Dog's chickens.

Bro Dog complains to Bro Nancy about what Hawk has done.

"Ah, Bro Dog," Anancy says, "you know how people say 'Trouble there up at bush, Anancy brings it come at house.' But you see how poor Bro Nancy doesn't do all the bringing."

Bro Dog says nothing.

MONKEY, TIGER
AND THE MAGIC TRIALS

At the time, King Monkey and family are the royal family. But, you see, no doors, no walls, no soldiers protect the palace.

Also, the palace of King Monkey and family is made without a single nail or piece of iron. All rock and wood, the great royal home is like a hill with trees around it. Sun shines and the palace glistens with the shining sun. Moon shines and the palace glistens with the shining moon. But a magic gold stool that is there glistens most of all.

You see, wrongdoers are punished, or set free, by the way ten Magic Stools work and make an answer.

Anybody may well think nearly all the Magic Stools are just bulky looking like ordinary small rocks. Or they only look like short pieces of cut up wood-trunk. But remember, the Magic Stools work together. They work in ways that only a certain kind of person can understand.

They are always there, at the back of the palace, in the open shed of the Trial Place. You see the Magic Stools all the same size, side by side, in a row, on bare ground. Nine of the stools are dark and crusty with age. But the last stool, the tenth one, standing at the end of the row, on your right, is gold – pure shining gold.

Puss-Cousin happens to come to the palace, to be put on trial. Puss-Cousin comes marched up by Chiefman Puss behind him like a policeman.

King Monkey comes down from his top room. He comes down serious looking. He wears a special dress. King Monkey walks into the shed, on the bare ground of the Trial Place.

Puss-Cousin is put to stand in front of the ten Magic Stools. King Monkey stands behind him, and speaks.

"Puss-Cousin," King Monkey says, "wrong has been done. You are here on trial. If you are guilty, you will die. If you are innocent, you will live and go completely free. Do you understand?"

"Yes, King," Puss-Cousin says.

"Good," King Monkey goes on. "I want you to count the Magic Stools. Point a finger at each one as you count. Let the Magic Stools speak. Count the Magic Stools. Now."

Puss-Cousin points with his finger and counts, "One. Two. Three. Four. Five. Six. Seven. Eight. Nine. Ten." Puss-Cousin drops dead, exactly as his voice touches the word ten.

King Monkey steps back in a kingly way. Chiefman Puss steps forward. He picks up the dead Puss-Cousin. He puts him across his shoulders. He bows to King Monkey. He walks away carrying Puss-Cousin. The other Puss-cousins and friends follow him to the burial. All this time nobody knows Tiger hides in the bush, watching.

On the very next day, Dog-Cousin is brought for trial. Dog-Cousin is put in front of the Magic Stools. King Monkey stands behind him and commands him to count. Dog-Cousin counts the Magic Stools and drops dead. Chiefman Dog steps forward to pick up Dog-Cousin to carry him away. Tiger bursts out from hiding. In his rushing in Tiger knocks people down. Tiger grabs up Dog-Cousin. Tiger runs mad-mad away with Dog-Cousin to make a meal of him.

Oh, everybody is shocked. People at the Trial Place are beyond themselves. Oh, the awfulness of it! People shout at Bro Tiger. People run after Bro Tiger. Everything only makes Bro Tiger run faster.

King Monkey calls, telling Tiger to come back. No Tiger comes back. The people band together and go searching the woods. No Tiger is found. Tiger gets himself well-well hidden. Everybody has to give up the search, thinking, "Oh, Tiger can't be seen. He looks no different from air!"

Yet Bro Tiger lurks about in hiding.

Unseen, Bro Tiger comes back close. He waits. He watches to see if another wrongdoer comes and counts the Magic Stools.

Tiger waits around for two days. No other wrongdoer comes. Tiger gets hungrier and hungrier. On the third day Tiger's hunger bites him hard-hard. Tiger sees two royal children playing. Tiger rushes out. Tiger grabs a royal Monkey-child and disappears with him.

With all the hunts and searches made, Tiger cannot be found.

Every third day or so, Tiger manages to make a meal of a royal Monkey-person. Tiger does that. Bro Tiger does that till King Monkey, Queen Monkey, children, servants are gone. Only one son and one daughter escape. And in great hurry-hurry they go looking for Mister Anancy.

All during that time, Bro Tiger is sitting on the throne, laughing. Bro Tiger thumps his chest. He laughs big laughs and says, "King Tiger. King Tiger. Tiger is King Tiger!" He roars, laughing.

Tiger roams through the palace from room to room. Tiger looks at himself in mirrors. He then pulls faces at himself and roars with laughter. Tiger sleeps in a different palace bed every night. Then, getting hungry, Tiger comes out looking for wrongdoers or palace visitors.

Visiting the palace, Rabbit-Cousin walks up.

"I'm in charge now," Tiger tells Rabbit-Cousin.

"You?" Rabbit-Cousin says, surprised.

"You are doubtful?"

"No, no," Rabbit-Cousin says, a little frightened.

"King Monkey's away on holiday," Tiger says. "Long holiday. Might not even be back. I see to all business here. I'm doing a prize. A big prize. Come. Follow me. I show you."

Tiger takes Rabbit-Cousin to the Trial Place and says, "D'you know what is gold?"

"Yes," Rabbit-Cousin says.

"Show me gold."

Rabbit-Cousin points to the gold stool.

"That's the prize," Tiger says.

Not knowing anything about the Magic Stools, Rabbit-Cousin is excited. With this unbelievable chance of winning such a big block of gold, Rabbit-Cousin says, "Really? That really is the prize?"

"It is the prize."

"And I can win it?"

"If educated enough. Go on. Try it."

"What do I do?"

"Count the stools. In one go. In one straight go. Do it, and point at them."

Rabbit-Cousin counts the Magic Stools and falls dead. Tiger is seized with shaking laughter. It's all so easy, he can't believe it.

Anancy hears about what is happening at the palace. Hurrying, Anancy runs into Old Witch. Walking quick-quick across shadows of sunlit trees, Anancy has no idea where Old Witch appears from. Old Witch stands in front of him saying, "Anancy, you need me. You need me."

"Mrs Old Witch, I'm in bad hurry," Anancy says.

"Where are you hurrying to?" she asks, walking beside him.

"To the palace."

"To do with the Magic Trials?"

"Yes."

"Ah!" Old Witch says, full of knowing. "D'you know something is badly wrong, Anancy? D'you really know?"

"Mrs Old Witch, I'm Bro Nancy. I'm here on my way."

"Oh!" Old Witch says, getting cross. "You're rebuffing me. Anancy, you're rebuffing me. Because you want all the praises for yourself. But – you need me. You really do."

"Mrs Old Witch, I'm in bad hurry, I say," Anancy says and walks away quick-quick.

"Magic spells can be broken!" Old Witch shouts with spite, left standing alone. "Magic spells can be broken, I say!" she shouts again.

At the palace, in a comfortable bed, Bro Tiger yawns and stretches himself. He suddenly gets up and comes out into bright sunshine. Bro Tiger sees Bro Nancy sitting against a tree near the Trial Place.

Getting up to meet Tiger, Anancy greets him sweet-sweet. "Good afternoon, Bro Tiger."

31

"What d'you want?" Tiger says. "I'm in charge here."

"Mister King Tiger, I see you are in charge."

"I'm glad you see that. I'm glad you see you should call me Mister King Tiger."

"Position can make a man a big-big man."

"I'm doing a prize, with the gold stool. You're good at good-luck, and a bit of brain. Come. Try it."

"You know I'm not an educated man," Anancy says.

"I get on. You see that. Copy me. Hear what I say. Win the gold stool."

Anancy laughs at how clever Bro Tiger thinks he has become. He knows Tiger believes he'll count the stools and die. But Anancy doesn't say he knows Tiger thinks that. Instead, Anancy says, "You mean if I win I'll have gold and be rich. And you will be a king already. So both of us can be proud and be good friends. Do you mean that?"

"Yes. Yes." Tiger answers without thinking. Impatient, he goes on. "Come on then. Come. Count the stools. All of them in one go."

Anancy counts, "One. Two. Three. Four. Five. Six. Seven. Eight. Nine. And one more."

Tiger looks up surprised, puzzled and then gets cross. "That isn't proper counting."

"All right, Mister King Tiger. It's not a time to burn yourself out getting vex. I can try again."

"Right. But better this time. Better this time."

Anancy counts again. "One. Two. Three. Four. Five. Six. Seven. Eight. And two more."

Tiger leaps up and stamps about in a rage. "Stupid, fool-fool man. Stupid, fool-fool man. Can't count! Can't count properly!" Tiger turns round in his rage, carried away with his anger. He points to the stools, saying, "Fool-fool man, count like this, One. Two. Three. Four. Five. Six.

Seven. Eight. Nine. Ten." Tiger drops down, rolls over, dead, showing his belly.

Anancy looks round, triumphant, expecting to see a crowd of happy faces praising and applauding him. Instead, Anancy sees Old Witch grinning, with a spiteful satisfaction. And there, caught in surprise, looking at Old Witch, Anancy hears a shuffling movement beside him. He looks and sees Tiger getting up.

Tiger gets up, dusts himself off and walks away.

Old Witch disappears, laughing, saying, "I told you spells can be broken. Broken! Broken! Broken!"

Since that time, palaces have doors and gate and walls and soldiers.

TIGER AND ANANCY
MEET FOR WAR

Tiger sends Anancy a message. The message says he's
coming round to Anancy's house to kill him. Anancy sends
back a message telling Tiger to come. He should come any
way he likes. But he should bring all his friends with him.
He, Anancy, will be waiting with all his friends.

Tiger arrives. Tiger comes like a king on horseback, with
weapons, with a crowd of Tiger-men around him. And every
man carries weapons of different kinds.

Tiger and his friends stop at Anancy's yard-gate. They
stop there. They see only one friend with Anancy in the
middle of the yard. They see nobody else. They see that Bro
Nancy has no weapon. They see his friend Bro Dog has no
weapon either. They see Anancy lying down with his head
on a piece of tree trunk.

They stand there at the gate. Bro Tiger and Tiger-men are
puzzled. They wonder what trick Anancy has planned. They
don't know what move to make.

Listen to the Anancy calling loud-loud. "Come on, Bro
Tiger. Come on. Don't torture me. Come and chop off my
head. Let the world know you are a brave-brave man. Let
my head drop like a block of wood."

34

Tiger feels a fool. Bro Tiger sits on the horse with his head all confused. Listen to Tiger now. "Bro Nancy? You know I have no intention to kill you. Why should you mistrust me?"

Hear the Anancy's reply. "Come on, Bro Tiger. Don't stretch out your brave deed. Don't make it a bad torture. Come and do what you come to do. If you don't do it today, you'll only want to do it tomorrow."

"Bro Nancy?" Tiger says in a pleading voice. "You know I'm not that sort of man. You know that." And Bro Tiger gets down from his horse. Bro Tiger gives up his weapons to the Tiger-men. Bro Tiger says, "I'm coming, Bro Nancy. I'm coming to shake hands with you. I want the whole world to know we are good-good friends."

"If you say so, Bro Tiger. If you say so," Anancy says. Then listen how the Anancy goes on wrapping up his words in tricky traps. "You invite yourself to my yard, I don't say, Go away. You want to shake my hand, I don't say, Oh no."

Bro Tiger steps through Bro Nancy's yard-gate. Bro Tiger sinks. Bro Tiger falls straight down into a pit concealed with dry leaves, and has rocks at the bottom.

Every Tiger-man is shocked. Every one clusters round the pit. Every one works and works to get Bro Tiger out.

Bro Tiger is lifted out. He is lifted out all battered up with limbs broken.

And Anancy and Dog see nothing of the Tiger-men's fuss over Tiger's bad outcome. Anancy and Dog did just leave, just go away about their business.

Anancy and Dog don't see it's a bandaged-up Bro Tiger the Tiger-men take away, take away on horseback.

All the same, that day hasn't changed Tiger. It hasn't stopped Tiger from giving Anancy a bad challenge.

ANANCY AND FRIEND

It's holiday time, you see. Everybody is dressed up, out in the village square. Out there too are cakes newly baked, sweets newly made, other things freshly roasted and fried and cool drinks wonderfully brewed. All have a strong sweet smell in the square.

Everybody eats and drinks and talks and laughs. Everybody is in a merry mood. Anancy has more than one drink of rum in his head. Dog has more than one drink of rum in his head too. The truth is, Bro Dog is tipsy. Every time Bro Dog drinks a little too much he becomes the biggest boaster you ever hear. So everything Bro Dog does now and says is a big show-off.

Anancy has to say, "You know, Bro Dog, you can go on as if you're really the wisest man."

"I'm no fool," Dog says, staring at Anancy. "I'm no fool. Not like some folks I could name. I can't help that. Can't help it I'm no fool, can I?"

"Perhaps you have more senses than everybody else, Bro Dog," Anancy says.

"I have," Dog says. "I always know I have more senses than most people."

"How many senses do you have?" Anancy asks.

"Every worker-part of my body is a sense," Dog boasts. "My nose is one sense. My mouth is another sense. My legs are two senses and my arms another two. My ears are two. My eyes are two. And my voice is another sense."

"So, Bro Dog, you have eleven senses," Anancy says.

Bro Dog counts up on his fingers. "Yes," he says, staring at Anancy. "Eleven!" Dog laughs. "And I know some people with none at all."

"Well, Bro Dog," Anancy says, "I have only two senses."

"Well, I'm sorry for you." Dog laughs and asks, "Which ones are your two senses then?"

Anancy says, "My first sense is, I KNOW ME; my second sense is, I KNOW MY FRIEND."

"Then I beat you," Dog says, laughing. Dog counts up and laughs out loudly. "I beat you by nine! By nine, Bro Nancy!" Dog rolls about laughing and repeating, "By nine, Bro Nancy! By nine...!"

Bro Nancy doesn't say a word.

Everybody says, "Never mind, Bro Nancy. Never mind. Your day will come. You'll have your laugh another day."

The very next afternoon, coming round a corner into a lane, Anancy gets a big surprise. There is Bro Dog frightened out of his wits! Tiger is holding him. Tiger has a firm grip on Bro Dog, ready to eat him.

Listen to Anancy now, talking like the best neighbour, all easy and carefree. "Good afternoon, Bro Tiger. So good to see you on a good afternoon with a good meal in hand."

Tiger is irritated. Tiger stares at Anancy with all his hate in his worst looks.

Anancy stands looking pleased, as if he'd like to honour

Tiger for holding Dog. "Oh, Bro Tiger," Anancy says, "you do have a meal that calls for a respectable man's thanksgiving. You must at least make the sign of the cross. And say grace for this good-good thing you're about to receive. Then, Bro Tiger, a passer-by like me can go his way in peace, feeling blessed."

Anancy has meant to make Tiger confused. And suddenly Tiger does look confused, and even shamefaced. Tiger always dreads looking silly or stupid or just ignorant. Tiger lets go of Dog and makes the sign of the cross on himself. Oh, Dog makes such a big, desperate leap from Tiger that he knocks him over. Just for a moment, open-mouthed, Anancy watches Bro Dog break away like a frightened thief, running for dear life.

Then swift-swift Anancy turns into Spider. Anancy shoots up into the near tree and is lost in branches.

Anancy and Tiger don't become better friends. But from that day, dog respects a sense of friendship.

ANANCY AND THE
HIDE-AWAY GARDEN

The garden belongs to Old Witch-Sister. Nobody is really
ever supposed to see this garden. But Anancy keeps on
hearing about the garden grown on rocks.

"It's the world's most glorious garden," people whisper to
Anancy.

"If allowed at all, not more than one stranger is ever supposed to see the garden," people also whisper to Anancy.

Anancy sets out alone to find the garden.

Anancy finds himself in a desert of rocks. He climbs up a
hillside of rocks. Getting up to the top, Anancy breathes like
a horse pulling hard.

At the flat top of the hill, the garden is open to wide blue
sky. Anancy stands fixed in surprise. Anancy is amazed.

"True-true. This is the richest garden in the whole world!"

Anancy whispers to himself. "The garden is growing, is fruiting, is ripening, is blossoming. Look at fattest vegetables! Look at shining fruits and flowers! Look at a garden of all reds, all oranges and browns, all yellows and purples!"

Anancy walks along the edge of the garden. Anancy can't help keeping on talking to himself. "What a garden of fat vegetables. What a garden of flowers that stay in your eyes. What a garden of little fruit trees ripening and blossoming. What a garden sweet-smelling of plenty-plenty!"

Anancy bends down. He examines the rocky ground. Roots are gone down, hidden in rocks, shaped like smooth mounds of earth.

Anancy stands. He looks in wonder at the colourful garden in bright hot sunshine. Anancy whispers, "Sunshine takes roots. Sunshine takes roots and grows like garden."

Anancy turns round. He goes back down the rocky hillside singing:

> "Sunshine 'pon rocks gets dressed up like garden.
> Sunshine 'pon rocks gets dressed up like garden.
> Seeds get wings in a breeze-blow.
> Seeds get wings in a breeze-blow.
> Catch them, pocket them, plant them back of house, O!
> Piece-piece luck comes quiet in one-one.
> Breeze-blow seeds raise up stone-land!
> Oh, catch them, pocket them, plant them
>   back of house.
> Oh, catch them, pocket them, plant them
>   back of house.
> Sunshine 'pon rocks gets dressed up like garden, O!"

Anancy stops singing. As he walks along, he begins to think again how the garden is rich and fat and colourful.

Anancy begins to think the garden should be his. He begins
to feel how it feels having the garden. Anancy begins to
count up what the garden can do for him. He reckons up that
the garden can get mountains of praises for him. And in the
heat of the day, he can lie back in a shade in the beautiful
garden. He can stay there and listen to birds singing, and go
off to sleep.

"Old Witch-Sister needs nothing beautiful!" Anancy says
aloud.

Then Anancy laughs a funny laugh of excitement. In
himself now he feels, he knows the Hide-Away Garden shall
belong to him – Anancy!

But, Anancy remembers – nobody can just take away the
garden, easily. For one thing, the garden has a Gardener-
man. He cares for the garden. He's also watchman of the
garden. Then, some mysterious ways work with the garden
that cannot ever be explained. Any food stolen from the
garden makes the eater keep being sick till the robber is
found out. Then, of great-great importance, there is the flute
playing by Gardener-man, who walks with a stick taller than
himself.

With his stick lying beside him, Gardener-man sits on
a comfortable pile of rocks at sunset every day. Sitting
there, he plays his flute to the garden. He gives the garden
his music till darkness covers him.

While the flute is playing, Old Witch-Sister always comes
and listens. Dressed in red completely, Old Witch-Sister
creeps up into the garden, unseen. Sometimes she just
listens and goes away again.

Other times, she begins to dance straightaway, on a flat
rock near the centre of the garden. But there is one big-big
rule, you see, that must be kept.

Gardener-man must never-never play his flute over a

certain length of time. If Gardener-man should ever go on with the music over a certain length of time, he will not be able to stop playing. Also, if Old Witch-Sister happens to be dancing, she too will not be able to stop dancing.

Anancy goes and sees his son.

"Tacooma," Anancy says, "I want you to get Bro Blackbird KlingKling to get nine Blackbird KlingKling-cousins together with himself. I want them to do a careful-careful clever job. I want them to hide, to listen, to learn Gardener-man's music of the flute, exact-exact. I want them to learn, to know, to remember every, every slightest bit."

The Blackbird-people creep up and listen unseen, as Anancy asks. Bro Blackbird KlingKling and cousins have sharp ears. They take in every sound of Gardener-man's flute music, quick-quick.

Anancy sends a message to Gardener-man. The message invites Gardener-man to come and eat with him. But, you see, Anancy goes and collects Gardener-man himself. And because he's setting a trap for Gardener-man, just listen to that Anancy. "Oh, Mister Gardener-man, I just happen to be passing this way. And my good memory says we are eating together. And as you know, Bro Nancy isn't a man to miss a friendly company a little longer. So I come and call for you."

Gardener-man walks with his stick taller than himself beside Anancy, towards Anancy's house. At this exact time, Anancy's son Tacooma makes his way to the Hide-Away Garden.

Quick-quick, Tacooma collects up some food from the garden.

Sunset comes. The Blackbird-people come and sit in Gardener-man's place, on the pile of rocks. The Blackbird-people begin to sing Gardener-man's flute playing, all to the garden.

The Bird-people work the singing in groups of three. When one group is stopping, the other group comes in smart-smart. Like that, the Blackbird-people carry on and on with Gardener-man's music, perfect-perfect.

With really sweet throats of the flute, the Blackbird-people sing and sing to the garden. Flute music fills the garden and the whole sunset evening, sweeter than when Gardener-man himself plays.

Dressed all in red, slow-slow, Old Witch-Sister creeps up into the garden. On her flat rock, Old Witch-Sister begins to dance, slow-slow. Her long red skirt sways about a little bit at first. The skirt begins to sway about faster. Then the skirt begins to swirl and swirl. From head to toe, with arms stretched wide, Old Witch-Sister spins and spins and spins. Darkness comes down. Darkness finds Old Witch-Sister swirling as fast as any merry-go-round.

Last to sing, on his own, Bro KlingKling takes over the flute-singing. As Bro KlingKling's voice spreads over the garden, Old Witch-Sister drops down dead, in a heap of red clothes. Then, at Anancy's house, Gardener-man is the only one to eat the stolen food from the garden. Same time as Old Witch-Sister, Gardener-man drops down dead too.

Anancy gets himself busy. Anancy sees to it that Old Witch-Sister and Gardener-man get buried as far apart as possible. He sees to it too that Gardener-man's walking stick is buried with him.

Then Anancy jigs about. Dancing, Anancy says:

> *"Sunshine 'pon rocks gets dressed up like garden.*
> *Catch them, pocket them,*
> *plant them back of house, O!"*

Anancy begins to plan making a feast for himself, family and friends. He begins to plan too how he'll get Bro Dog, Bro Pig and Bro Jackass to work the garden.

Next day, early-early, Anancy starts out with Dog, Pig and Jackass and others to see the Hide-Away Garden.

They come to the garden. Anancy cannot believe his eyes. Every fruit and vegetable and flower and blossom is dried up. Every leaf is shrivelled and curled crisply. Anancy whispers, "The whole garden is dried up. The Hide-Away Garden is dead. Dead! Really dead!"

Anancy sings:

> *"Whai-o, story done, O!*
> *Whai-o, story done, O.*
> *The garden dead.*
> *The garden dead.*
> *The garden dead, O!"*

Everybody is sad. Even people who have never seen the garden get sad and very sad.

"That should never ever happen again," people say.

Nobody likes people who play bad tricks.

TIGER AND THE STUMP·A·FOOT
CELEBRATION DANCE

Everybody really waits for Tiger to arrive. Bro Tiger is to come and challenge Bro Nancy as best dancer. But people enjoy themselves.

People dance inside the hall of bamboo-roof. People dance outside, in the yard of palm trees. Music rushes out of the hall, frolicking round the moonlight yard of people.

The dressed-up musicians sitting, playing in the village hall, have good fun. They grin. They nod to the beat. Every musician plays hard to play sweeter music than the other.

Bro Puss rubs his fiddle bow on strings, busy-busy. Bro Puss doesn't care at all his violin is chipped and tatty. And dressed like Mrs Puss, Bro Puss has the inside of his mouth capped, to look like he has no teeth. Bro Monkey rolls his head about, hitting his drums. Like his wife, Bro Monkey is padded to look humpbacked. Nodding hard, Bro Goat rocks about shaking maracas. Like his wife, Bro Goat wears a head-mask and looks like he has a bashed-in head. Bro Rabbit plays his flute, moving it from side to side. Like his wife, Bro Rabbit wears a black eye-patch. Strumming so swift-swift, Bro Dog plays his banjo like he wants to hurt himself. Like Mrs Dog, Bro Dog looks one-legged. Bro Pig, with eyes shut, rolling his head about, plays bass-fiddle. Dressed too like his wife, Bro Pig wears a snout-mask, making him look like half of his mouth is bitten off.

Everybody has come dressed up, looking like disfigured people. The hall has walls that are only halfway up, you see. And there are no doors. The music escapes freely. Dancing there in lantern light, dancers can see other celebration-people outside, in the moonlight yard of palm trees. People dance and talk and laugh.

You see, it's the big Celebration Dance that's on. Listen to what the custom is, all who doesn't know.

Once a year the dance happens. It's put on to allow people to become the same. That is, become like other people who have a dropped body-part, and have something missing or faulty. If you have no limb or eye or anything faulty, you can still come to the dance; but you have to make yourself look like you've lost something.

Nobody knows how disabled-looking Bro Tiger will arrive. Nobody knows how Tiger will look. Bro Tiger and Bro Anancy's dance challenge is the biggest happening of the celebration evening.

Like sweet friends, Anancy and Mrs Rabbit stand in the moonlight yard. In her long white dress, Mrs Rabbit looks marvellous. Of course for her disablement Mrs Rabbit wears her black eye-patch too. Opening her one-eye wide on Anancy, Mrs Rabbit asks uncertainly, "Is Bro Tiger going to come? Bro Tiger's never been to a stump-a-foot dance before, surely, Mister Anancy?"

"True, Mrs Rabbit," Anancy says with a shy face. "True-true. But, Bro Tiger will come." Anancy shuffles on his one leg. Then Anancy remembers he feels he's best dressed. He remembers he has on a stiff white front, with a cut-away black suit. Also, he has on his watch-and-chain hanging down. Anancy pulls himself up proud-proud and goes on talking. "If Bro Tiger's scared of a swift dancing foot, in the company of a wooden one, dressing up is even harder for poor Bro Tiger. But if hiding-away beats him, Bro Tiger well knows Bro Nancy becomes the winner."

"Bro Tiger likes himself looking strong-strong. Doesn't he?"

"True-true, Mrs Rabbit."

She goes on. "I'm sure Bro Tiger doesn't even like to dress up looking like he has a missing part."

"Clear vision," Anancy says, looking at Mrs Rabbit. "You can see deep-deep. All the same – not to miss my good-good chance – shall we go and dance?"

"Certainly, Mister Anancy. Certainly."

Anancy dances with his one-leg and crutch-stick. Mrs Rabbit dances looking out of one eye. People laugh at one another. People go on dancing, all around the hall, inside and outside. With their half-of-heads and half-of-faces, their one-eyes and one-ears, their one-arms and one-legs, they bob up and down and sway themselves and jig about. Now and then somebody tumbles over, and everybody laughs.

The music plays on and on. Then the music stops.

People crowd round Bro Anancy.

"Is Bro Tiger going to come, d'you think?" one-eared Bro Jackass asks.

"D'you ever know Tiger to just give up as loser against Bro Anancy?" Anancy asks, leaning on his crutch-stick.

Nobody answers. Instead, standing with Anancy's son Tacooma, Bro Blackbird KlingKling looks out of his one eye and says, "What loss-of-limb will Tiger come with to do his dance?"

Bro Dog answers sharp-sharp, "If Bro Tiger should come having ten legs, he'll still have no legs to stand on against Bro Nancy."

Everybody laughs.

Mrs Anancy comes up, brisk-brisk. Using lantern light, Mrs Anancy and other women have been busy cooking in little outhouses at the back of the hall. Mrs Anancy asks Anancy to put out more bucketfuls of drinks.

Though the people around Anancy want to talk to him, he leaves them standing. He leaves even truly disabled cousins, like One-Legged Peacock, Broken-Wing John Crow, Dropped-Leg Goat, Broken-Mouth Patoo and others.

Sitting down, standing up, people chatter. But everybody eats. Mrs Anancy and Dora, Tacooma's wife, and other helpful women serve food, inside and outside.

Smells of hot steaming food settle on the night. Steaming bowlfuls after bowlfuls go around. It's peppery soup with pounded vegetables and plantain fried. It's spiced-up barbeque meats and freshly baked bread. It's boiled pudding and rum-and-spice cake. It's more and more of all sorts of spicy nut cakes.

Full of food and drink, feeling good, Bro Dog does two clever tricks in front of the musicians' stand. Then again, unexpected, Bro Dog leaps up in the air, spins like a ball and falls great-great, on one leg. Oh, Bro Dog loves his big applause and praises! Rabbit recites a funny poem about Owl falling off a branch while having a daytime dream. Bro Anancy tells two funny jokes, one about himself and Tiger. Bro Pig gives a loud belch. Then, on his one leg, without a stick, Peacock does a strutting dance, perfect-perfect.

But biggest uproar of laughing comes when Alligator creeps in late, missing every bit of food. Alligator's disablement gets lots of laughing too.

Alligator wears a thin stretchable pink suit. Alligator wears the skinfit suit to make himself look like he has lost his thick leather-skin.

Just before midnight everybody comes in from outside. They all come in and cluster together with everybody else. Something different is going to happen!

A new mood has come. Everybody is frightened, but happy-happy with it.

You see, at midnight the Three-Legged-Horse is supposed to appear. It usually happens at every Stump-a-Foot Celebration Dance.

Everybody knows the Three-Legged-Horse isn't any ordinary ghost-horse. Everybody knows it's a duppy-horse – a really bad-bad ghost-horse. It will just blow off one big snort on you and kill you – anybody – for nothing!

All the same, not everybody can see the Three-Legged-Horse. But, there is agreement. All people who can see it agree. The Horse has one back leg missing. All agree that its tail, its mane, its whole body, is white like pure moonlight. Pure moonlight! But most of all everybody knows that in the presence of the Three-Legged-Horse, nobody – nobody – must ever talk. Nobody must ever say one single word.

The musicians begin to play and sing:

"Bro, O Bro,
People, O people,
if you see it come—
'pon three legs or 'pon one—
say not'n',
say not'n',
only quiet-quiet,
only quiet-quiet.
Bro, O Bro,
People, O people,
if you see it come—
with three eyes or with one—
say not'n',
say not'n',
only quiet-quiet,
only quiet-quiet,
        only quiet-quiet..."

The musicians go on and on and on repeating the song. Then they stop, sudden-sudden. Everybody knows the Three-Legged-Horse has arrived. The place is total silence. The people who can see it, see the Three-Legged-Horse. They see it come in backwards, moving in reverse, up, towards the musicians. They know it never turns round. It will go up and down the hall in a straight line.

Slowly, swishing its moonshine tail, dipping its moonshine head, it goes up the hall. Clop-pi-ti. Clop-pi-ti. Clop-pi-ti. It stops. It turns its head and looks at the people clustered on each side. It goes again. Clop-pi-ti. Clop-pi-ti. Clop-pi-ti. It stops again, looks on both sides then goes again. Clop-pi-ti. Clop-pi-ti. Clop-pi-ti.

As before, swishing its moonshine tail and dipping its moonshine head, it comes down frontways quicker. Clop-pi-ti, clop-pi-ti, clop-pi-ti. It looks both sides. It nods its head. It swishes its tail. Twice again it does its clop-pi-ti, clop-pi-ti, clop-pi-ti.

Then, at the hall entrance, the Horse disappears with the speed of a bird. As if he would smash up the country road in a terrible runaway clattering of hoofs, the Horse is gone like a hundred mad horses in the night.

Its clattering goes. The echo fades away. Everybody is relieved. Everybody talks crazily. The people touch one another, shake their heads and wave their arms about. They drag their hands over their faces. They rub their hands together. They scratch themselves. They laugh. They sing. They whistle. The people go on as if they are happy to be alive after something awful. But they are also stopping themselves from saying even one word about the Three-Legged-Horse. Everybody knows not one single word is ever to be said about the Horse.

So the people do all kinds of antics with their hands. And they talk nonsense. They go on like this:

"Did I ever come here tonight?"

"Oh no, no, no. But it's the brightest, brightest, bright moonlight."

"Did we eat? Did we eat tonight, last night, last week?"

"No, no, no. Last week I put no clothes on."

"Hoh, hoh, hoh! You do ask something you know I can't remember."

"We might as well have come without our heads."

"Don't you know? Don't you know we're here without heads?"

The people slap each other playfully and laugh. They go on like that. Nobody remembers the night is still far from over.

Sudden-sudden, Tiger rides into the hall on horseback. People have to leap out of the way, quick-quick. Tiger makes the horse dance about. Tiger has done nothing to make himself look disabled. Instead Tiger is dressed up like a plantation overseer. Tiger wears sun-helmet and riding breeches fitting tight down to his ankles. And he has his riding whip.

In the saddle, Tiger holds the reins of the horse strong-strong and stiff. He makes the horse arch his neck, dancing round the hall. More and more people move out of his way. Tiger makes the horse trot round, doing dance movements.

Unexpectedly, Bro Puss strikes up his fiddle-playing. And the whole band starts up playing. Tiger and the music get the horse to dance in with the beat. Everybody starts clapping to the beat as well. With Tiger on, the horse dances round and round the hall like that. Then sudden-sudden Tiger turns the horse round and gallops away, mad-mad into the night of moonlight.

Everybody can hardly believe what has happened. Bro Nancy is struck dumb, for once. People don't know whether to laugh at Bro Nancy or be sorry for him. But everybody – everybody – just laughs and talks and tosses their arms about with the joy – the sudden-sudden happening that Tiger put on. Everybody knows Bro Tiger has taken Bro Nancy by surprise and outsmarted him.

All the same, listen to the Anancy.

"Friends! Friends! That is a no-contest. A no-contest!" And the Anancy stretches out his arms wide. "Friends, I'll challenge Bro Tiger again. I'll challenge him again. And next time – next time – he'll be on his own, on his own-own two legs."

"Good idea," everybody shouts, laughing. "Good idea!"

So people begin to wait. People begin to wait for that next time when Bro Nancy and Bro Tiger will clash in a dance challenge.

MRS ANANCY,
CHICKEN SOUP AND ANANCY

Mrs Anancy has six chickens she fattened up to sell. She wants the money to get a dress to wear to a special church service. Anancy makes himself believe Mrs Anancy has enough nice dresses already.

Anancy whispers to himself, "Oh, those fat and lovely chickens! They'll be much, much nicer in one special meal. Any good and loving husband deserves that. Any one! But, oh, there is the trouble. Mrs Anancy will never, never agree."

Bro Nancy works out a way for the six fat chickens to become his meal.

Anancy goes and sees Bro Dog. Anancy gets Bro Dog to agree to go and do a little trick job for him.

Bro Dog goes and hides himself in the doctor's surgery. He stays there hidden till the surgery is closed.

Just before night comes down, Mrs Anancy walks into her home. She comes and finds her husband close to death, in pain.

"Oh, my husband, what's the matter? What's the matter?"

"Oh, my wife – good-good wife – pain has me in its jaws. Pain chews me up. Pain cuts me up. Everywhere." Anancy clutches himself and rolls about in the bed.

"My poor-poor husband. Where is the pain? Where?"

"Everywhere." Anancy groans. "In my belly, in my throat, in my mouth, on my tongue, there's a blazing fire."

"I must get the doctor," Mrs Anancy says, all worried.

Anancy groans. Anancy sobs. Anancy gasps, "Wife – I'm getting a glimpse – a glimpse – of another world. A light – a light beckons me to another place."

"No, no, husband. Don't go." Mrs Anancy embraces her husband. "Hold on. Hold on. I'm going to the doctor. Right away. Right away."

Anancy keeps up his tired groans. Then, as Mrs Anancy is ready to rush out of the house, he says, "Good wife, you must hurry. But – but – but I'm getting terrible signs. Please. Please don't take any short cuts. No short cuts, good wife. None. There are pits hidden. There are trees with roots loosened. There are rocks on hillsides, propped by few rotten leaves."

"Every word is taken, good husband. Every word is taken. Now I must go." Mrs Anancy leaves the house in haste.

Then sudden-sudden Mrs Anancy stops. She doesn't want to leave Bro Nancy alone. She looks back at the house. A little way further along she looks back at the yard. In disbelief, she sees Bro Nancy rush out onto the road. He goes the other way, hurrying. He turns in on to the short cut.

Mrs Anancy is puzzled. She turns round and follows Anancy.

At first Mrs Anancy is worried. Her husband may be driven by his illness to do something crazy. Then she realises he's surely heading for the doctor's surgery. Wondering what Bro Nancy is going to do Mrs Anancy follows unseen. And to keep up with his speed she has to put in bursts of running.

At the surgery the place is closed. Then Bro Dog comes out and receives Bro Nancy. Both go back inside and lights are put on. Mrs Anancy stands outside in shocking disbelief. Nothing is wrong with her husband. He and Bro Dog talk happily inside.

Not knowing exactly what to do, Mrs Anancy stands outside waiting and thinking for a while.

Then Mrs Anancy goes to the surgery door and knocks. Doctor comes and asks her in.

Doctor is a bearded and bent-back little old man. Doctor wears dark glasses and a white coat. Doctor speaks in a peculiar croaking voice.

"It's my husband, Doctor," Mrs Anancy says. "He's at home in bed in terrible, terrible pain."

"Does he have pains everywhere?" Doctor asks in his peculiar croaking voice.

"Yes, Doctor."

"The pains come worst in the belly and throat and mouth and tongue?"

"Yes, Doctor."

"Common. Very common." Doctor shakes his head. "Some bad-bad cases about."

"Will he be cured, Doctor?"

"Yes, yes. Completely. But there's only one cure."

"Yes, Doctor? Tell me."

"Chicken soup. Go home, Mrs Anancy. Find six to eight of the fattest chickens. Make the tastiest soup you ever made. Give every bit of it to the patient, every bit of flesh and soup and seasoning. And leave him alone to eat, madam. Leave him alone."

"Thank you, sir."

Mrs Anancy conceals herself outside. She sees the surgery lights go out. She sees Bro Nancy and Bro Dog slip away smart-smart.

Mrs Anancy gets home. There is singing inside. She stands. She listens to every bit of Anancy's song:

> *"A big-big good lot*
> *Can make you fat-fat.*
> *Why be one of you*
> *And not two of you?*
> *Why be one of you, O?*
> *And not two of you, O? . . ."*

Wanting Anancy to hear her, Mrs Anancy goes inside noisily. Instant-instant, the singing stops. She goes into the room. Anancy rolls about, groaning in pain.

"Any news? Any good news, good wife?"

"I'm to give you chicken soup."

"That'll cure me?"

"I'm to give you lots of it. Lots of it."

"Oh! Oh!" Anancy groans. "When will the treatment start?"

"Not tonight."

Early morning Mrs Anancy goes and sees Dora. She comes back, kills the six chickens and begins the cooking.

Mrs Anancy makes herself very busy. Importantly, she goes and opens Anancy's bedroom window. Mrs Anancy sets up her cooking just outside, under the window. The cooking steams up more and more. Tempting cooking smells drift in and fill Anancy's room.

With the delicious cooking under his nose, Bro Nancy turns and twists. He turns his face to the wall. He turns his face the other way. He turns his face towards the ceiling. Sometimes Bro Nancy sits up in bed. When he hears Mrs Anancy round at the back, he craftily takes a peep outside at the cooking.

Anancy lies down. Part of his song comes into his head:

> *"A big-big good lot*
> *Can make you fat-fat..."*

Mrs Anancy sets up a long table outside, near her cooking. She goes and closes Anancy's window. She tells him, "I don't want to tempt you any more. I don't want you to either see or smell the spiced-up soup. Everything is ready. Just wait."

Anancy continues his long wait.

Unseen by Anancy, Dora arrives with a party of village children. Dora settles the twenty-four children around the long table. Picked out as the worst fed, they wait with ravenous appetites.

Mrs Anancy dishes up every bit of the chicken flesh and soup and seasoning. All is put in front of the children. In no time every bit is eaten up. Every bowl is left clean.

Tortured by sounds outside, and his waiting-waiting, Anancy leaps up, swings the window open and rushes outside.

Anancy sees the children and their empty bowls. He sees the big empty iron pot. He sees everybody looking at him. Anancy holds his head and screams, "My chicken soup! My chicken soup!"

The children burst out singing:

"*A big-big good lot*
Can make you fat-fat.
Why be one of you
And not two of you?
Why be one of you
And not two of you?
Anancy, O!
Anancy, O!..."

Anancy storms out of the yard. But he doesn't stay away for long. He is simply too hungry.

RATBAT AND TACOOMA'S TREE

Spiderman Tacooma wants to be more than just being called the son of the great Anancy. He doesn't find that easy. All the same, on his own Tacooma can make strange happenings work, like magic.

Tacooma will sit under his fig tree and watch sunrise. He'll watch midday sun and watch the moon come up at midnight. Tacooma loves to sit and watch and listen or just think.

Tacooma will think on things like – the way an ocean lives there in the seabed it has; the way darkness is the only world of deep-sea fishes; the way fire is able to make itself burn; the way a seed changes more and more into a tree; the way webbed feet of flying frogs open out in flight like four little umbrellas...

Tacooma is sitting under his tree, listening to birds in it, and thinking. Then, from the little house next door, Ratbat his neighbour comes and complains about the noise in the tree that Tacooma sits under.

In his deep thinking, listening to the birds, Tacooma is surprised.

But Bro Ratbat and his Ratbat-people sleep in the daytime!

Unable to sleep, half sleepy, and not able to see properly in the bright afternoon sunshine, Ratbat has to come out wearing dark glasses.

Ratbat stands in the village road and complains loudly. He is cross about the feasting and frolicking of the noisy birds in Tacooma's tree. The birds' noise is keeping everybody awake in his house, Ratbat says.

It's true, the birds do carry on. The birds squawk and squeak and scream. And some coo, some caw, some cheep; some twitter, some whistle, some chatter, some gossip; some laugh, some cry; some sing prettier than the feeling tree-blossoms give off in sunlight.

Tacooma has been listening to those very different sounds the birds make.

"Listen to the noise!" Ratbat says. "Just listen to it! Beats me how some people think nothing, miserable nothing, about anybody else."

Tacooma explains that the crowd of birds only feasts and frolics because figs are ripening.

"Anyway," Tacooma says, "Bro Ratbat, you've never complained before."

"Past history!" Ratbat says. "All past history. These days noise gets to me. Noise shakes up my brains. It has to stop, Bro Tacooma. It has to stop. I can't stand it. I can't stand it..." Ratbat carries on complaining.

All the Ratbat-people come out on to the village road, wearing dark glasses. They flap their arms about complaining that hard-working night people can't have any proper rest. The Ratbat-people go on and on until they decide Tacooma's tree must be cut down.

"My tree!" Tacooma says. Tacooma stands up. "My tree! My tree will never be cut down."

"It will be put down," Ratbat says. "Big and bulky as it is, your tree will be cut flat – on its side!"

Hearing the argument some of the birds come down onto low branches, listening.

Bro Blackbird KlingKling arrives and says he and friends will collect up soft feathers to stuff all the Ratbat-people's ears.

"No Ratbat-person wants to sleep with ears corked up," Ratbat says.

Bro Woodpecker says he and friends will come and fit better doors and windows to Ratbat's house.

"No Ratbat-person will want to try to sleep with building noise around everywhere. Everywhere!"

Bro Nightingale says he and friends will come and surround Ratbat's house with singing.

"No Ratbat-person has ever slept any sweeter in Nightingale's singing," Ratbat says.

Sudden-sudden, Bro Nancy appears on the scene.

Bro Nancy holds his arms high up over his head and says, "Stop! Everybody, stop!"

There is silence. Complete silence.

"There'll have to be a decision," Anancy says. "There'll have to be agreement."

"Surely, there has to be a decision," Ratbat says.

"Agreed," Tacooma says.

Anancy begins with his order. Anancy says, "One–Tacooma must stop the noisy birds in three minutes' time. Or stop them tomorrow.

"Two–Ratbat must cut down the tree within three minutes. Or within three days."

Bro Tacooma begins to argue.

"No argument," Anancy says. "No argument whatsoever is allowed."

"Nobody can axe down a big tree in three minutes. That's crazy," Ratbat says.

"Nobody's going to axe down my tree in three days either," Tacooma says.

"Long before three days," Ratbat says, "it'll be down on its side – flat!"

Before Anancy disappears he calls Tacooma to one side. Quietly he says, "Tacooma, you didn't have to argue. You know you didn't have to. You know you have good friends who'll always defend you like sharp claws and teeth. You know that, don't you?"

And, as Anancy has whispered – reminding Tacooma he has friends to call on – the secret friends arrive. Like a small army, tough little trees come and make a strong fence around Tacooma's big tree.

Standing close together, looking like part rock, part wood, part weaponry, some guardian trees are covered purely with thorns sharp like cockspurs. Others also have thistle leaves needle-like as any porcupine's back. Others also have leaves of stinging nettles.

Next day at dusk, Ratbat comes through Tacooma's gateway with his six Ratbat axe-men carrying axes and machetes. They face Tacooma's tree. And the Ratbat men are stunned. They stand staring. They can't believe they see a tough guardian barrier right round Tacooma's tree.

Ratbat looks at his Ratbat axe-men. Everyone is alarmed. This fierce army didn't stand round the tree yesterday. And – it seems – nobody is at home.

Loud and cross, Ratbat calls, "Tacooma!"

There's no answer.

He calls again. "Tacooma!"

There's no answer.

"Where's that Tacooma?" Ratbat shouts. "Come on. Let's attack. Attack!"

The Ratbat men chop the guardian trees. But every time a Ratbat man chops, a branch bends quick-quick and lashes back, like claws, beaks, thorns and nettles together. Ratbat men chop; they're hit back. They chop, chop, chop; they're hit, hit, hit. They begin to itch. Except Ratbat himself, everyone drops weapons and begins to scratch tummy, legs, back, arms, neck, and all over.

Ratbat shouts, "Come on, attack! Attack!"

Ratbat men again chop, chop, chop and are hit, hit, hit. They notice their axes and machetes are blunted. And itching bites them. They fall about scratching themselves. Ratbat alone chops wildly taking his hits. Then Ratbat stops, and scratches and notices his axe is blunted. He finds every weapon is blunted as if it chopped a rock. Ratbat sees everybody bleeds and scratches. Ratbat himself bleeds as he scratches.

The Ratbat-people hurry away shouting and scratching their tummies and backs, legs and arms and everywhere.

Next day Ratbat comes back with fresh Ratbat-people.

Again he shouts, Attack, attack! Again they are hit. Everyone falls about scratching and bleeding. Again they hurry away shouting and scratching all over.

On the third day, Ratbat is bandaged from head to toe as he goes about begging for help. Nobody wants to be bandaged as he is. Nobody joins Ratbat to chop down Tacooma's tree.

Darkness comes down. The fourth day comes. Nobody sees a single thorn, thistle or nettle bush around Tacooma's tree that is still standing there.

From that day ratbats set up home in caves to hide from daytime noises. Anancy has a hand in the happening.

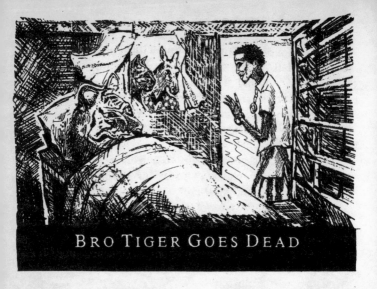

BRO TIGER GOES DEAD

Tiger swears he's going to crack up Anancy's bones once and for all.

Tiger goes to bed. Bro Tiger lies down in his bed, all still and stiff, wrapped up in a sheet. Bro Tiger says to himself, "I know that Anancy will come and look at me. The brute will want to make sure I'm dead. He'll want to see how I look when I'm dead. That's when I'm going to collar him up. Oh, how I'm going to grab that Anancy and finish him!"

Bro Tiger calls his wife. He tells his wife she should begin to bawl. She should bawl and cry and wail as loud as she can. She should stand in the yard, put her hands on the top of her head and holler to let everybody know her husband is dead. And Mrs Tiger does that.

Mrs Tiger bawls and bawls so loud that people begin to wonder if all her family is dead suddenly and not just her husband.

Village people come and crowd in the yard, quick-quick.

66

Everybody is worried and sad and full of sympathy. The people talk to one another saying, "Fancy how Bro Tiger is dead, sudden-sudden."

"Yes! Fancy how he's dead sudden-sudden. All dead and gone!"

Anancy also hears the mournful death howling. When Anancy hears it, listen to the Anancy to himself. "Funny how Bro Tiger is dead. Bro Tiger is such a strong and healthy man. Bro Tiger is such a well-fed man. Bro Tiger is dead and I've heard nothing about his sickness."

Anancy finds himself at Tiger's yard, like the rest of the crowd. Straightaway, Anancy says to his son, "Tacooma, did you happen to hear Bro Tiger had an illness?"

Tacooma shakes his head. "No, no. Heard nothing at all."

Anancy goes to Dog. "Bro Dog, did you happen to hear Bro Tiger had an illness?"

Bro Dog shakes his head. "No, no. Heard nothing at all."

Anancy goes to Monkey and Puss and Ram-Goat and Jackass and Patoo and asks the same question. Everyone gives a sad shake of the head and says, "No, no. Heard nothing at all."

The crowd surrounds Anancy. Everybody starts up saying, "Bro Tiger showed no sign of illness. Death happened so sudden-sudden, Bro Nancy. So sudden-sudden!"

Anancy says, "Did anybody call a doctor?"

The people shake their heads and say, "That would have been no use, Bro Nancy. No use at all."

"Before death came on, did Tiger call the name of the Lord? Did he whimper? Did he cry out?"

"He didn't have time, Bro Nancy. He didn't have the time," everybody says. "It was all so sudden."

Listen to Anancy now, talking at the top of his voice.

"What kind of man is Tiger? Doesn't Tiger know that no good man can meet his Blessed Lord sudden-sudden and not shudder and cry out?"

Tiger hears Anancy. Tiger feels stupid. Tiger feels he has made a silly mistake. Bro Tiger gives the loudest roar he has ever made.

Anancy bursts out laughing. Anancy says, "Friends, did you hear that? Did you hear that? Has anyone ever heard a dead man cry out?"

Nobody answers Anancy. Everybody sees that he is right.

By the time Bro Tiger jumps out of the sheet on the bed to come after Anancy, the Anancy is gone. Bro Nancy is well away.

Nobody even talks to Bro Tiger now. Everybody just leaves Bro Tiger's place without a single word.

ANANCY RUNS INTO TIGER'S TROUBLE

Going about his business, Anancy hears a sound. Anancy stops. Anancy listens.

The sound is heavy breathing.

Someone must be having a struggle. Somebody must be trying hard to do something difficult. Anancy turns and goes towards the sound.

It's Bro Tiger! It's Bro Tiger – trying to climb out of a deep pit. Anancy can see the top of Tiger's weary head dipping with his tired breathing.

Anancy's own head spins in dread and excitement.

What can he do? It's too much to ignore Bro Tiger!

He always wants to crush him up. Bro Tiger always wants to have him in pieces, always wants to have his body-bits round his nose.

Anancy bends over the edge of the pit.

Tiger is near the top. Poor Bro Tiger is tired. Bro Tiger is gripping on to parts of tree roots and a rock. His legs spread about in different ways. And, oh, Bro Tiger is thin! Bro Tiger is getting to look like an empty sack from days of hunger. He must have been in the pit for days.

Anancy sees the work of Tiger's attempts to get out. Tiger's feet have raked a fresh track along the side of the pit all the way down to the bottom. Anancy thinks, "Oh, poor hard-working man Tiger! Poor fallen-down-the-pit Bro Tiger has worked hard to get out! Bro Tiger has been stuck in the pit here. This is why Bro Tiger hasn't tried to kill him lately. This is why nobody brings him news that Tiger lurks about waiting for him!"

Sudden-sudden, Anancy gets a great idea.

Anancy puts on his sweet-sweet voice and says, "Oh, Bro Tiger, it's you! Fancy it's you, Bro Tiger. Looking so different from usual. Looking so, so unrespectable!"

Surprised to see Anancy, and tired and panting, Tiger says, "Yes, Bro Nancy. It's me. It's me, Bro Tiger."

Listen to the Anancy now. "Were you coming to see me, Bro Tiger, when this oh so terrible falling-down-a-hole happened and so battered you up?"

"Bro Nancy," Tiger pants, "I'm so weak – I feel so bad – so weak – all memory's gone. Gone. Gone away."

"Oh, poor Bro Tiger!" Anancy says, with his voice all sugary. "Such a beautiful man, a powerful man, turned into a striped bag of bones! But never mind. You're almost free, Bro Tiger. You see you're almost free. Almost out of the pit. You can see that."

Tiger groans. Tiger grunts. Tiger says, "Don't know. Don't know, Bro Nancy. Have been up here before. Only to slide down again."

"Don't give up," Anancy says. "It's not like you to give up."

Tiger tries. Tiger struggles. Tiger makes another big move to get himself out of the pit. But tired, Tiger's breathing is loud. Oh, Tiger's breathing is loud. Then Tiger manages to say, "Can't move, Bro Nancy. Can't move any more. Too hard. Too hard. What – what can I do?"

"Pray, Bro Tiger," Anancy says. "Pray. Pray hard. Put hands together and pray."

Tiger lets go, putting his paws together. Tiger slides down, down, right down to the bottom of the pit again.

Anancy lies down on his tummy. Anancy hangs his face over the edge of the pit and calls, "Are you all right, Bro Tiger? Are you all right down there? I'd come and keep you company but I don't want to become your dinner. Is that all right, Bro Tiger?"

No answer comes from Tiger. But Anancy knows Tiger will not give up. He knows Tiger will get out. He knows Tiger will be working out ways to catch him, to gobble him up.

Anancy remembers he has left home to go on business. Anancy steps off, quick and brisk. Anancy walks away fast.

71

Mrs Dog First-Child and Monkey-Mother

Mrs Dog's first-child is clever, you see. From when she is small-small she can stand on her head and catch things with her feet. Swing-Swing will catch a big unhusked coconut with her feet, her lovely little dog-child's feet. Lots and lots of difficult acts Swing-Swing-Janey can perform for herself alone, or for a crowd.

Then one day, just before sunset, Monkey-Mother happens to see Swing-Swing-Janey playing alone.

Passing by, going home with her tribe of many children, with one on her back, Monkey-Mother stops. She stands there with child on her back, watching Janey.

Swing-Swing carries on. Swing-Swing is in front of her house, there at roadside, practising her sticks-catching.

Swing-Swing tosses up four sticks and catches them. She

72

keeps on doing that. Monkey-Mother is thrilled. Monkey-Mother grins. Monkey-Mother puts down her child and settles down watching, with all her lots of children around her watching too.

Then so excited to have a crowd watching her, Swing-Swing-Janey starts up something different.

Swing-Swing tosses her ball up, then falls quick-quick on to her hands, throws her bottom end up, catches the ball with her feet, bends her knees, flicks the ball up again, half spins back onto her feet and catches the ball with her hands.

Seeing Swing-Swing's movements so precise, so perfect, the family grin and clap. And grinning and clapping Monkey-Mother says:

> *"O so right and so spry,*
> *So nippy and so flippy!"*

And grinning and clapping her lots of children say:

> *"O so right and so spry,*
> *So nippy and so flippy!"*

Swing-Swing-Janey repeats her act. Then Swing-Swing does lots of other things she can do.

The sun sets, and nobody sees Janey. Swing-Swing has disappeared.

Night comes down. No Swing-Swing-Janey is anywhere. Mrs Dog stands outside and calls and calls; no answer. No Swing-Swing comes home.

Mrs Dog practically goes off her head with worry.

Mrs Dog walks quickly to every neighbour and asks about Swing-Swing. Nobody has seen her child. Mrs Dog approaches everybody passing her house. Nobody has seen Swing-Swing-Janey. Nobody knows to where the child has disappeared.

Then just before bedtime, Mrs Puss calls and says, "I hear you lost your child. I have to say I did see your child. Monkey-Mother carried away your child. They all joked and laughed together, walking on and on together, like a friendly family."

"But where does Monkey-Mother live?" Mrs Dog wants to know.

Mrs Puss has no idea. Nobody knows where Monkey-Mother lives. She roams about; it is known. She lives miles and miles away; it is believed.

Mrs Dog begins to go about looking for her child, promptly.

Many strange villages see Mrs Dog for the first time.

Mrs Dog sees tailors making clothes, shoemakers making shoes, tinsmiths making vessels. Each time Mrs Dog asks the people, "Have you seen a dog-child with Monkey-Mother?"

"No," they say.

"Do you know where Monkey-Mother lives?"

"No," they say.

Every person or group of people Mrs Dog meets she asks the same questions and gets the same answers.

Mrs Dog keeps on going with her travelling and her looking. Other strange villages see Mrs Dog for the first time.

She sees basketmakers making baskets, carvers carving wood, potters making pots. Each time Mrs Dog asks the people, "Have you seen a dog-child with Monkey-Mother?"

"No," they say.

"Do you know where Monkey-Mother lives?"

"No," they say.

Every person or group of people Mrs Dog meets she asks the same questions and gets the same answers.

Mrs Dog keeps on going with her travelling and her looking.

Strange fields see Mrs Dog for the first time.

Mrs Dog sees people picking coconuts, she questions them. She sees people cutting stems of bananas, she questions them. She comes to an orange grove and sees people picking oranges. She says to the orange-pickers, "Have you seen a dog-child with Monkey-Mother?"

"Yes," they say. "Two days ago. We saw them mango-picking. The dog-child caught the mangoes picked and dropped. Sometimes she caught them with her hands. Sometimes she went down on to her hands, kicked up her feet and caught the mangoes and put them in the basket."

Anxiously, Mrs Dog wants to know where the mango trees are.

The orange-pickers tell her where.

Mrs Dog finds mango tree after mango tree but sees nothing of Swing-Swing or Monkey-Mother.

Mrs Dog goes home.

Mrs Dog weeps and weeps. Mrs Dog misses her first-child oh so much! And Mrs Dog is tired. Mrs Dog and husband and family wonder and wonder, "What may have happened to our Swing-Swing-Janey? Eh? Whatever may have happened to our little Swing-Swing?"

One after the other, everybody remembers how Janey has many busy antics, and makes them laugh. They remember how she comes to getting her name, Swing-Swing, from her father, from her leaping up to low tree branches and swinging from one to the next.

Mrs Dog starts out on her travels again.

A new river sees Mrs Dog.

She sees men in a canoe, river-fishing. She calls out, "Have you seen a dog-child with Monkey-Mother?"

"Yes," they say. "One hour ago they came back from the other side of the river. The dog-child swam and pulled the raft with Monkey-Mother and family."

Anxiously, Mrs Dog asks, "Where does she live? Do you know where Monkey-Mother lives?"

"Yes," the men say. And the men explain in detail where Monkey-Mother lives.

Mrs Dog comes to a rocky barren place. No trees are here. There are only rocks and hills of rocks.

Mrs Dog stands outside a kind of house of rocks.

Monkey-Mother and children come outside, into the yard.

Monkey-Mother waves her arm about and says, "She's not here. She's not here. Go away. Go away. I tell you—"

Before Monkey-Mother is finished speaking, Swing-Swing comes round some rocks, carrying wood. Monkey-Mother grabs her. She pushes her, bundles her round to the back, and locks her in.

"I want my child," Mrs Dog shouts. "I want my child!"

Monkey uncles and aunts and cousins all come out waving their arms about, telling Mrs Dog, "Hop it! Clear off. Get away. And don't you come back!" Oh, the Monkey-people are noisy and threatening!

Mrs Dog suddenly feels lonely and bullied. Mrs Dog feels bullied and lonely and hopeless and can't help crying. Mrs Dog begins to turn away.

The Monkey uncles and aunts and cousins carry on waving about and shouting, repeating, "Hop it! Clear off. Get away. And don't you come back!"

But, you see, just as the fishermen tell Mrs Dog where Monkey-Mother lives, they also tell Bro Nancy and Bro Dog. So, they arrive!

Listen to the Anancy straightaway, talking like the best of friendly visitor.

"To Mrs Monkey-Mother and all, a good-good and abundant afternoon!"

"Good afternoon, Mister Anancy," Monkey-Mother says, in a quiet voice.

Anancy notices everybody has gone quiet and goes on. "I know, there is no need to say, to most respectable strangers, good citizens come to meet good citizens not as a crowd, but in a small-small number of two."

"We are respectable people too, Mister Anancy," Monkey-Mother says.

"That's exactly why none of you can bark? Can any of you bark?" Anancy asks.

"No, sir," Monkey-Mother says.

Anancy knows the moment has come to let Swing-Swing hear him. At the top of his voice, Anancy shouts, "Well – who can bark, let her bark!" Anancy goes on even louder. "Bark now who can bark!"

Swing-Swing-Janey yelps, perhaps forgetting she can bark. Then Swing-Swing begins to bark like wild and crazy, like a terrible hollering in everybody's ears.

Looking badly shamefaced, Monkey-Mother holds her head down.

"Mrs Monkey-Mother, will you please let out the dog-child and let her come to us?" Anancy commands.

Monkey-Mother says nothing. Monkey-Mother only goes slow-slow and shamefaced and lets out Swing-Swing.

Swing-Swing-Janey comes to her mother, Mrs Dog.

Oh, child and mother are happy!

From that time, mothers don't like their children to get too friendly with strangers.

ANANCY AND STORM AND THE
REVEREND MAN-COW

Hurricane wrecks the whole countryside, you see. Almost
everything and everywhere is flattened and flooded. Nobody
is without damaged property. Anancy has his kitchen
chopped in two by a tree fallen across it. And the sky stays
gloomy.

Anancy-Spiderman is sad.

Anancy walks out with Mrs Anancy through the village.
He sees only storm-battered houses and trees and everything
and everywhere.

Anancy goes on and looks at his own lands.

Anancy finds his coconut and banana trees, his climbing

yam-vines on upright sticks – his fields of crops – are flattened. Some of his animals are dead.

"Oh, it feels bad to feel sad," Anancy says to his wife. "It feels so, so bad to feel sad."

"Husband, the sun will shine again," Mrs Anancy says.

"Wife, I can't believe how I can't believe that," he says.

Going back home, Anancy can hardly walk. Anancy and Mrs Anancy stop on a seat called Travellers Rest. The seat is fixed against a fig tree that grows and spreads itself in a stone wall.

"Wife," Anancy says, "an idea has come into my head. And I think it will help me get over my sadness."

"Will the idea really work?" Mrs Anancy asks.

"If I can get Bro Monkey to do a little job for me, the idea will be a wonder. It'll work so very, very well."

"Will Bro Monkey agree to do the little job?"

"Bro Monkey won't disagree," Anancy says. "Bro Monkey won't know everything. Bro Monkey shouldn't know everything. And he won't."

Now, Bro Monkey is sad about the hurricane too. But Bro Monkey is by himself, thinking. Bro Monkey is sitting right there, with his back against the same wall as Anancy. They don't see each other. But Bro Monkey hears all that Bro Nancy says. And right away Bro Monkey is suspicious, but waits to see what Anancy will ask him to do.

Brisk-brisk, Bro Nancy starts to work on his idea.

First of all, Bro Nancy sends a most urgent message to the Reverend Man-Cow, asking him to come and see him.

Quick-quick, the Reverend Man-Cow arrives in his long gown, carrying Bible and prayer book.

Anancy sits down on his veranda with the Reverend Man-Cow. And oh, the Anancy-Spiderman is sad. Listen to the Anancy:

"Oh, Mister Reverend Man-Cow, I don't know what to do. I'm not a man to feel so bad from feeling sad. It is a sadness that is a woeful hurtfulness. All my days have gone to waste. Even food has no taste. Sir, I don't eat. I have nothing to feel good with. I have nowhere, sir, nowhere, to draw anything nice from. All I have is feeling bad-bad from feeling sad. I try and find not one song will start in me. Any goat, sir, even the breeze, can break through me like a weaky-weaky fence. Hunger can kill me, 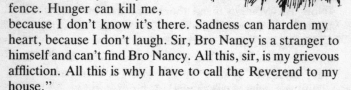 because I don't know it's there. Sadness can harden my heart, because I don't laugh. Sir, Bro Nancy is a stranger to himself and can't find Bro Nancy. All this, sir, is my grievous affliction. All this is why I have to call the Reverend to my house."

"Oh, dear, dear Bro Nancy! I understand," the Reverend says. "It's the storm, good brother. It's the hurricane that has created such a disaster in you and affected you."

"That's it, sir," Anancy says. "It has smashed up my kitchen and smashed up my field and smashed up everybody's everything."

"Yes, Brother Anancy. The Lord giveth and the Lord taketh."

"But, sir, why does he have to take so much?"

"Remember. You mustn't question the works of the Lord. You mustn't question."

"It will still be in my head, sir."

"Brother Anancy," the Reverend Man-Cow says, "I will pray for you. Let us pray."

The Reverend prays for Anancy. As the Reverend says, "Amen", Bro Nancy bursts out crying, saying, "Mister Reverend, I feel worse. I feel much, much worse."

"Then I will pray for you again."

"Perhaps, later, sir. For now, can we talk? Can I ask you something?"

"Yes. Ask me something."

"Mister Reverend sir, since your prayer didn't work I'm asking you to do something else."

"Ask me, Brother Anancy," the Reverend says. "Ask me."

"I'm asking you to put on a festival."

"A festival?"

"Yes, Reverend. A Festival of Shining Things. I'd like nobody else but you to be in charge of a Festival of Shining Things!"

"Why? Why a Festival of Shining Things?"

"Sir—most Reverend, Reverend sir—in my condition of loss, I don't want back only my beautiful fields. I long for plantations and estates and vineyards. I don't want back only my sound kitchen. I long for a Great-House or a mansion. For food crops I lost, I don't want back only a dinner. I want feast after feast to refill me."

"Keep heart, Brother Anancy," the Reverend says, "I understand your loss. I understand your longing to have something back. But how—how will a festival help?"

"Oh, sir—most holy Mister Reverend Man-Cow—the Festival will spread out all our shining things before my eyes.

The things will put a light into my heart, into my blood, into my body. The things will brighten eyes and hearts of all Brothers and family and everybody. Every eye will see we have things the storm did not touch."

"Splendid! Splendid!" the Reverend says. "I will do it. I will take it on. I will organise your Festival of Shining Things."

"Thank you, Reverend," Anancy says. "Thank you." But that was not everything. He Anancy alone must decide on certain arrangements.

For one, Anancy insists that all the Shining Things that people bring must be put on the spare bed in his and Mrs Anancy's bedroom.

On his side, the Reverend Man-Cow insists that on the day of the event, until it starts, Anancy should stay at his son's house; that people will bring their Shining Things on the same day of the Festival; that no name will be put on anything; that after everybody has seen everything on show, there'll be a thanksgiving prayer and song; and that everybody will file in afterwards and take back their own things.

Anancy goes off and sees Bro Monkey.

Anancy finds Bro Monkey cutting his son's hair in the backyard. Bro Nancy and Bro Monkey go and stand to one side together and talk privately.

Bro Nancy still doesn't know Bro Monkey has overheard his conversation with Mrs Anancy. And Bro Monkey isn't going to let on. Yet Bro Monkey isn't going to say no. Bro Monkey is going to handle matters in his own way.

Anancy tells Monkey the Festival will open just before night comes down. When it is dark enough Mrs Anancy will be in her bedroom getting dressed. At that time everybody at the Festival will be locked out and kept away from the room with the Shining Things. At that time, exact-exact,

Bro Monkey is to slip in through the backdoor, pick up all the gold pieces – the rings, the bangles, the earrings, etc., and again slip away.

Anancy insists on how Bro Monkey should remember that at the time – when it is made known to everybody that Mrs Anancy is getting dressed – everybody should see that even he isn't allowed in. He'll try to get in the room. But it will be arranged with Bro Dog that Bro Dog should stop him.

Last of all, Bro Monkey should remember, Bro Nancy isn't asking him to pick up wood, to pick up leather, to pick up shell or silver. Only gold. Only gold will wash away the sad-sad disaster self that cloak up Bro Nancy.

Bro Monkey asks nothing about a reward for his helping to steal the gold. But Bro Monkey asks, "What shall I do with the gold pieces when I have them outside?"

"Hide them," Bro Nancy says. "Hide them. Till everything cools down."

"But everything won't cool down. The loser of the valuables – and everybody else – will keep on wanting to know what's happened to them."

"Rely on bad memory," Anancy says. "Rely on bad memory."

"Suppose everybody's memory stays good and sharp? And all eyes fall on you, Bro Nancy?"

"Bro Monkey, eyes fall on me Bro Nancy?"

"Yes, Bro Nancy. Suppose eyes fall on you – as guilty?"

"Bro Monkey, dear-dear Bro Monkey, you mustn't put questions into my blank space. Just think of how you spoil everything. Spoil everything! Bro Monkey – I tell you – it's gone. I clean forgot you asked that question. Tell me you forgot you asked that question."

"Bro Nancy, we'll talk again."

"No. No, Bro Monkey," Anancy says. "When business is settled, business is settled."

Bro Monkey goes to see Bro Dog.

Bro Monkey finds Bro Dog clearing up his storm-damaged backyard.

Bro Monkey explains how Bro Nancy wants him to steal the gold at his Festival.

"Then we must spoil his plan," Dog says. "We must spoil it."

Dog and Monkey decide that Dog will take it on to let something unexpected happen at the Festival of Shining Things.

On the day, Mrs Anancy's green silk cloths – and gold one on her spare bed – are soon crowded with things people bring. So many things are brought, Mrs Anancy finds she has to put down her patchwork cloths on the floor round the room as well.

Anancy comes into the room.

Anancy sees that his bedroom is transformed into a wonderful place of Shining Things displayed. To Anancy, everything is truly wonderful.

Anancy's eyes are drawn first of all to gold and silver necklaces and pendants. His wide-eyed look moves over horn, silver and gold rings, over little boxes of beads, little boxes of gold sovereigns and boxes of rare silver coins.

Glowing with pleasure, Anancy's roving eyes gloat over large and small ornamental baskets with embroidered fancywork, decorated calabashes, decorated fans of bamboo and of straw, coconut-shell ornaments, painted nut marbles and stones, seashells of all sizes and shapes, alligator and goatskin bags, decorated sandals, decorated walking-sticks, little figures in carved wood, calabash and leather masks, decorated clay bowls and mortars-and-pestles, silver plates and spoons and forks, the many embroidered cloths and children's dresses.

Anancy's eyes glint with excitement. Anancy bursts out singing:

> "You come, breeze-blow –
> Whai-O! Breeze-blow!
> You trample-trample all of out-of-doors.
> You chuck down rooftops down 'pon floor.
> You churn-up treetops into mud.
> You leave birds without a word.
> You flood crabs from out of holes –
> Yet you find no silver, you find no gold.
> You come, breeze-blow –
> Whai-O! You come, but had to go.
> You find no silver you find no gold.
> You find no silver you find no gold..."

Anancy's house becomes like a garden-party of people. Everybody is dressed up and shows best behaviour with nicest words. Everybody smiles and touches one another and talks. The clusters of people go in and out of Anancy's room, looking at and liking every Shining Thing. People keep shaking Anancy's hand. They say, "Oh, Mister Anancy, you've lifted our hearts with your Festival." "Bro Nancy, it's good-good you're singing again." "Mister Anancy, you deserve every piece of Shining Thing in your room." "Shining Things, Bro Nancy, next time we'll ask you to get the moon for us and bet we'll have it."

Anancy is pleased. Reverend Man-Cow is pleased. Every contributor and visitor is pleased. All go on looking at things and smiling and touching one another and talking till darkness comes down.

Then Anancy begins to get fidgety. Anancy can't keep his mind on his conversation with people. Anancy's head is full of the gold he wants Monkey to steal for him.

Anancy goes and closes his bedroom door. He asks everybody to stay out of the room and allow Mrs Anancy to change her dress.

A minute or so, after Anancy closes his bedroom door, Dog rushes up to the locked door and calls in his loudest voice, urgently, "Mrs Anancy! Mrs Anancy!"

"Yes," she answers inside the bedroom.

"Your cakes in the oven outside exploded and burst into a hundred pieces! Come, please! Come and see to your cooking, quick-quick!"

Mrs Anancy comes out of her bedroom in a hurry, leaving the door wide open.

Bro Monkey comes forward, letting Anancy see he's not able to take any gold.

The crowd of people quickly drift back into the room. All over again, they start looking at the Shining Things, while touching one another and talking and laughing.

The Reverend Man-Cow comes into the room. The Reverend opens his wide arms and calls everybody to hymn-singing and prayer.

Thanksgiving over, and the eating starts, everybody keeps on thanking Bro Nancy for the wonderful Shining Things idea.

Bro Nancy sits and smiles and smiles, lapping up the sweetness of the praises.

Good people have always owed much to the help of their friends.

ANANCY AND DOG AND PUSS AND FRIENDSHIP

Bro Puss insists on doing the shopping, even when he's not at all fit and well.

Anancy sees Bro Puss walking down the road with a stick. Anancy can't believe it's Bro Puss with leg all bandaged up, hobbling towards him, carrying a shopping basket.

Anancy stops.

"Oh, Bro Puss, I'd say good morning. But all so hurt and bandaged up, how can it be a good morning for you?"

"You take notice, Bro Nancy," Bro Puss says. "You take notice. All the same, good morning, Bro Nancy."

"Good morning, Bro Puss. But – what bad luck has overtaken you with so much pain?"

"Ah, Bro Nancy! It's nobody else besides Bro Dog."

87

"Bro Dog? Bro Dog has damaged you?" Anancy is shocked.

Sad-sad, Bro Puss looks down. He nods his head and says, "Yes, Bro Nancy. Bro Dog has damaged me. Bro Dog has actually broken my leg."

"Just out of sudden badness?"

"Well," Puss says, "as you know, me and Mrs Puss share our home duties. And few days ago, I went to the shop. I waited. I then happened to point out I was first to be served. Bro Dog jumped on me. Held me. Tossed me against the wall. Next thing I knew I couldn't get up. Couldn't raise myself, Bro Nancy. Then I saw I couldn't walk at all."

"Oh, maddest madness!" Bro Nancy says. "Crazy madness! That's not like the Bro Dog I know." Bro Nancy shakes his head. "Not, not at all."

"But it is, you know," Puss says. "It is. Bro Dog's like that. I know. I know from experience."

"Bro Puss," Anancy says, "I'm sad. I'm sorry. Sorry to hear. Sad to see you like this. But – it's here in me, it's not like Bro Dog to be so vile. I have to believe a bad-bad tiger spirit rose up in Bro Dog and made him vile. Made him damaging."

"No, Bro Nancy. No," Puss says. "It's just him. It's just Bro Dog. It's just him... All the same – can you speak to him?"

"Speak to him?" Anancy says. "I'll go right now. I'll let Bro Dog answer to this damage he's done to you."

As Anancy speaks, his son Tacooma comes along. Tacooma says good morning to his father and Bro Puss and agrees that Dog has behaved very, very badly.

Tacooma takes the shopping basket from Bro Puss and walks to the shop with him. Anancy goes off straight to see Bro Dog.

Listen to the Anancy now, sitting down all friendly-friendly. "Bro Dog, I met a man today. You may call him Bro Kitten. And you know what has happened to Bro Kitten?"

"No," Dog says. "What?"

"Bro Lion has broken Bro Kitten's leg."

"Badness," Dog says. "Terrible badness! Lions are all the same. Wild and ignorant. What else can you expect? They get no schooling whatsoever. None."

"Bro Dog," Anancy says, "suppose I should say, the Bro Kitten is Bro Puss. And the Bro Lion is you. What would you say?"

Bro Dog goes quiet. Then Bro Dog says, "I'd say, I'm ashamed. Badly, badly ashamed."

"Ashamed enough to make the broken leg come good?"

"I can't mend broken legs. I can't, can I?"

"No, Bro Dog," Anancy says. "But you can mend a lot-lot by becoming friends."

"Me getting friendly with Puss? After breaking his leg? Would you even talk to me?"

"Bro Puss himself asked me to come and talk to you," Anancy says.

"Really?" Dog says, guilty and surprised, looking round at Anancy.

"Yes," Anancy says. "He asks me to come and talk to you."

Again Dog goes quiet, then says, "It's not the first time I hurt Bro Puss. You know that."

"Yes, Bro Dog."

"Yet," Dog says, "it seems Puss knows I feel bad I damaged him."

"Suppose," Anancy says, "both of you should meet, eye to eye, not too cross, cool-cool, with only a little bad-mind?"

"Would be all right," Dog says. "Would be good. If you can fix it up."

Anancy works as a go-between. Anancy gets the badness between Dog and Puss really cooled off. It even seems all their trouble has gone – disappeared.

Everyday now Bro Dog goes to the house of Bro and Mrs Puss. He gets wood for them. He gets water. He fetches and he carries practically everything. By the time the leg of Puss is healed up again, he and Dog are perfect-perfect friends.

Bro Dog and Bro Puss are seen together everywhere, doing jobs, or just enjoying themselves like old friends.

One day, Bro Dog invites Bro Puss to come to the seaside with him. Bro Puss hesitates, not really wanting to go, but still not wanting to be the first to refuse a friendly request.

They go to the seaside.

Dog promptly slips into the sea and begins to swim and dive and do all kinds of things in the water, enjoying himself. Puss sits under a coconut tree and watches Dog.

Bro Dog waves to Puss, calls him, "Come on in! Come on. The water's great!"

"I'll stay here and watch you," Puss calls back.

Every now and then Dog calls to Puss inviting him to come in the water. People on the beach become amused by Bro Puss and Bro Dog.

Every time Dog calls to Puss to come and try doing this or that, Puss calls back saying, "I'll stay here and watch you."

And Puss sits there and watches Dog float, dive, leap out and splash back in the water and swim in all different kinds of ways.

As Dog comes out of the water, Puss compliments him on being such an excellent swimmer.

"Anybody can do it," Dog says. "Anybody – who isn't frightened."

"It's a talent you have," Puss says, "and I don't. That's why I sit and watch you."

"Oh, come off it," Dog says. "Anybody can swim. Anybody who isn't frightened."

Bro Puss changes the subject. Bro Puss says nothing more about his lack of talent and feeling for enjoyment in water.

A few days later, at a holiday time, Puss specially invites Dog to a packed lunch at a well-used picnic and beauty spot.

Not having eaten, on purpose, Dog arrives hungry. All ravenous and ready to tuck into the special feast-lunch both Mrs and Bro Puss prepared together. Yet, Bro Puss hangs about, in no hurry to open up the lunch and begin the eating.

Sitting there under a tree, Bro Dog has to wait, listening to long drawn-out tales Bro Puss tells about his family.

Then, sudden-sudden, Bro Puss picks up the well-stuffed bag of food. He tosses the handle round his shoulders. He fastens himself against the tree. And, calm-calm, Bro Puss climbs himself up and up into the tree. Soon, Bro Puss is sitting at ease, comfortable, in the branches of the tree, with the bag of food.

At first, Dog doesn't understand what is happening. He's puzzled at what funny game Puss is playing. Bro Dog stands, looking up into the tree.

Bro Puss looks down and calls, "I have lunch for you, Bro Dog. Come and get it."

"What d'you mean?" Dog says. "You know very well I can't get up there. And you must know my belly's rumbling."

"Anybody can climb up," Puss says. "Anybody who isn't frightened."

Dog is shocked. Dog remembers using those words at the seaside. Dog looks down, thinking, "Oh! Puss is playing a game of teaching-a-lesson. Puss wants to trick me into seeing something!"

Dog is cross. Dog feels he has been tricked. He feels he has been invited to a special lunch so that he can be taught a lesson. Dog thinks back at the swim in the sea.

Dog remembers he hasn't made a call to Puss for a swim to put him down or to give him any lesson. He has made his call to Puss to come and swim – come and enjoy the swim with him – as he has felt it.

"Things are natural when they happen as they happen," Dog tells himself. "When something happens between friends as you feel it, that's natural. But when a game is set up to catch you out, or teach you a lesson, that's a trick."

Getting hungrier and hungrier, Dog walks round the tree, looking up, and says, "Bring the food down, Bro Puss. You invite me to lunch. Come down with it."

"Come up and get it, Bro Dog," Puss says. "Climb up and get it. Anybody can do it. Anybody – who isn't frightened."

Dog sees that Puss is sitting comfortably in the tree eating his lunch.

Dog leans against the tree. Dog sits down. Dog feels like waiting just to attack Puss when he comes down, and not bother with any of the food. But Dog is so empty, it hurts.

Dog knows he cannot leave the food. Dog knows too, he cannot find it in himself to attack Puss and eat his food.

Suddenly, Puss comes down from the tree. Puss hands Dog his lunch.

Standing there, Dog takes the lunch, looking really cross with Puss. A wave of madness comes over him to attack Puss. But, instead, an enticing smell of the cooked meat under his nose makes Dog want to eat more than attack Puss.

Dog sits down. He looks up crossly at Puss, sitting there. Bro Dog picks up the enticing meat; he gobbles it, crushing up the bones. And Bro Dog goes on eating his way through his lunch, not saying a single word.

"Have you got the point, Bro Dog?" Puss says. "Do you see now...that different people can do different things? And...we have much more...because different people can do different things? We have bird-singing...and frog-croaking. We have cow-mooing, and jackass-braying. We have horse-galloping, and kangaroo-jumping...Say you see the point. Come on, Bro Dog. Say you see the point. Some people can get about in water...Others can get up and around in a tree...Say you see my point. Say you see it!"

Dog finishes his lunch, gets up and says, "Bro Puss, if ever we are going to manage being friends, we better keep it on the ground. And not in the sea or up in any tree. All right?"

Bro Dog walks away quickly by himself, going off in a huff.

From that time, cats and dogs keep trying to be friends.

ANANCY AND
BAD NEWS TO COW-MOTHER

Cow-Mother is at her yard, eating alone. Anancy comes.
Anancy disturbs Cow-Mother, saying, "Good morning,
Cow-Mother."

Cow-Mother looks up surprised. "Oh! Good morning,
Mister Anancy."

"And how are you this late morning," Anancy goes on.

"I'm very well," Cow-Mother says. "I'm very well."

Anancy's face and Anancy's voice all go sad-sad as
Anancy says, "Cow-Mother, oh, Cow-Mother, you are not
really very well at all."

"Of course I'm very well," Cow-Mother insists. "Why
then, Mister Anancy, d'you tell me I'm not very well?"

"Cow-Mother," Anancy says, "you'll see you're not at all very well, when you know Tiger is coming to butcher you."

"What? Heavens above!" Cow-Mother says, in great alarm. "What are you saying? Is this true? Is this really true?"

Anancy nods. "Yes, Cow-Mother. Yes. Bro Tiger's coming to make meat of you. Only just a little later today."

Cow-Mother well knows Anancy has a way of finding out everything.

In great shock and horror and worry, Cow-Mother calls Cow-Daughter and shouts the terrible news.

Cow-Daughter comes, all shaking in terror and dread.

Cow-Mother and Cow-Daughter begin to beg Anancy, "Oh, Mister Anancy! Bro Nancy. Dear-dear Mister Bro Anancy! You must help us. You have to help us. Come on. Say you'll help us!"

Anancy well knows he has a plan worked out already. But listen how the Anancy shows himself careful-careful.

"Well," Anancy says, "I can only try. I can only try. But if I only try, it'll still be a hard-hard try."

"Try for us, Mister Anancy," Cow-Mother and Cow-Daughter say. "Try for us with a hard-hard try."

"Well," Anancy says, "to try and help, I have to use a little plan."

"Use the plan," Cow-Mother and Cow-Daughter say. "Tell us the plan. Tell us. Ask of us anything."

"Well," Anancy says again, "when Tiger comes, Cow-Daughter has to be left with Tiger, alone."

Cow-Daughter is thrown into panic. Cow-Mother yells in horror, "What! Leave my daughter with Tiger? Never. Never! How can I do that? Do you realise, Mister Anancy, that my young daughter is with child? Do you realise that?"

"Cow-Mother," Anancy says, "you should worry. But hear

95

Anancy. Stay cool-cool. Cow-Daughter will not turn into Tiger's flesh and Tiger's blood."

"How will you stop that? Just how will you stop that?" Cow-Mother asks, all beyond herself with worry.

Anancy begins to explain. Cow-Mother and Cow-Daughter stand quiet-quiet and listen.

Anancy explains that with his plan, mother and daughter have to be separated. Cow-Mother can come and hide away on his land. To pass the time away, Cow-Mother can occupy herself digging mounds of yam-hills.

Anancy takes Cow-Mother and walks her round a whole acre of his land to be dug. And Anancy gets Cow-Mother started on the digging of yam-hill mounds before he leaves.

At Cow's Yard, waiting alone, always looking out, trembling, Cow-Daughter sees Tiger coming up the track to her place. Tiger is arriving, coming, walking all slow-slow.

As Tiger comes into Cow's Yard, he hears Anancy's voice. "Good afternoon, Bro Tiger. And the very best of good afternoon!"

Tiger turns his face upwards and sees Anancy sitting in a tree branch over him.

Surprised, annoyed, irritated, Tiger asks crossly, "Where's Cow-Mother? I can't see Cow-Mother."

"Your sight is good-good, Bro Tiger," Anancy says. "Cow-Mother is away. But Cow-Daughter is here. Cow-Daughter is here, growing bigger and bigger for you every minute."

"Who says I want to wait on anything growing?" Tiger says.

"Ah! I see," Anancy says. "Bro Tiger can't wait. Does Bro Tiger know how people say, 'Can't-Wait Bro Tiger isn't at all Mister Bro Tiger'?"

"What d'you mean?" Tiger asks with a serious face.

Anancy knows Tiger will listen. Anancy knows Tiger hates to be seen as dim or stupid. Anancy knows he must engage Tiger and impress him and confuse him. Listen how the Anancy goes on.

"Can't-Wait Bro Tiger isn't at all Mister Bro Tiger. Can't-Wait is little boss of hungrybelly, ruling-ruling everybody, making Bro Tiger lose out in the end. Oh, so lose out in the end!"

"Lose out?" Tiger says. "How can I lose out? I never lose out. No little idiot can make me lose out. But – how d'you know people talk about me?"

"Bro Tiger – you are a thinking man. Think, Bro Tiger. Think."

"I'm a thinking man," Tiger replies crossly. "I think. I always think."

"Then, Bro Tiger, you should see, that rich man and clever man never eat big-bulk and big-bulk and big-bulk."

Tiger doesn't think whether that is really true or not. Tiger only goes silent. Then, softly, Tiger says, "There's something in that." And Tiger sits down.

The Anancy goes on. The Anancy puts it over on Tiger that rich man and clever man eat only nice dainty-dainty little lots of food.

Tiger suddenly says, "Anancy, I walked here with a total-total empty belly. I still have it."

"Of course, Bro Tiger," Anancy says. "Of course. But remember, you've eaten lots and lots of big-bulk before. And you walked here with a total-total empty belly. Rich man and clever man eat little dainty-dainty bits. And I never, never, heard a rich man or clever man complain of walking with empty belly."

Tiger is silent. Then Tiger says, "There's something in that." Tiger turns his face up towards Anancy in the tree and says, "Anancy, you think I don't know things, don't you? You think I'm stupid? I'm not stupid."

Anancy sweetens up Tiger. He assures Tiger how he's far, far from stupid. Then Anancy tells Tiger how it's because people know he knows things why Cow-Daughter has gone through the trouble to prepare and keep a special dinner for him.

"Special dinner for me?"

"Yes, Bro Tiger. For you."

"Where's the dinner?"

Cow-Daughter, who all this time has kept herself locked up, calls out, telling that Tiger's dinner is in the kitchen.

Anancy comes down from the tree and goes with Tiger and finds the dinner. It is in a big wooden bowl on the kitchen table. The dinner has a spoon with it, and a pot of flowers beside it.

With Anancy watching him, Tiger sits at the kitchen table and eats up the food.

Anancy calls Cow-Daughter to come and shake hands with Tiger.

At first Tiger is all shamefaced, shy and reluctant to shake hands with Cow-Daughter, but eventually does.

Cow-Daughter goes and brings out a big dish of whole pudding and gives it to Tiger, with a spoon. Standing where he is, Tiger polishes off every bit of the pudding. Cow-Daughter turns her back to get him a mug of water. Tiger chuckles at how silly the big dish of sweet pudding makes him feel.

Anancy points out to Tiger that he can stay with Cow-Daughter and get regular meals.

Tiger chuckles, telling he prefers to have the job of watching Cow-Daughter getting bigger and bigger. Then Tiger chuckles at himself, again saying he'd like to watch himself everyday to see if the eating of high-up food makes him turn into a better man.

Tiger stays on with Cow-Daughter.

Anancy makes regular visits to Cow's Yard, at all sorts of times. He also goes and gives news to Cow-Mother regularly.

At first, if Cow-Daughter is cooking, Tiger is there watching her. If she is washing or ironing or doing anything in the yard, Tiger is there watching her.

Cow-Daughter sees that Tiger likes her cooking. She gives Tiger all kinds of extra and in-between titbits.

Tiger begins to help. Tiger gets wood. Tiger gets water. Tiger fetches and carries and does whatever task Cow-Daughter gives him.

One day when Cow-Daughter is coming up the hilly slope of the yard, carrying some food from the garden, Cow-Daughter gives birth to a baby. Suspecting that something is the matter, Tiger comes and finds that Cow-Daughter's baby has rolled halfway down the hillside. Cow-Daughter is by far too weak to move.

"Bro Tiger, please get my baby," Cow-Daughter asks him.

Tiger trots down the hillside, collects the baby, gives it to Cow-Daughter and helps her to get inside the house.

By now, Cow-Mother has dug all of Anancy's land into mounds of yam-hills. She has also organised his little hut and made it clean and tidy. Anancy has been taking all the news about Cow-Daughter, but Cow-Mother is anxious-anxious wanting to go back home.

Out on one of his regular walks these days, Tiger suddenly remembers how Cow-Daughter has become smaller, instead of going on getting bigger. Tiger doesn't understand that having had her baby – and no longer being pregnant – Cow-Daughter has reduced in size.

Sudden-sudden Tiger thinks how marvellous it would be without having to bother about Cow-Daughter. To be free of Cow-Daughter seems a most wonderful idea.

Tiger doesn't return to Cow's Yard at all.

Tiger leaves. All the same, Tiger turns away from Cow's Yard with a little malice in his heart against Anancy. Tiger feels Anancy has somehow tricked him. Bro Nancy knows that. Bro Nancy keeps his eyes wide open for Tiger.

Mrs Puss, Dog and Thieves

Bro Dog falls into hungry-time, bad-bad.

Bro Dog is starved. Every day Bro Dog gets thinner. Hungry-time reduces Bro Dog to almost skin and bone. Bro Dog's knees knock when he walks. All knock-kneed and tottering, all looking and feeling terrible, poor Dog goes on down the road and comes face to face with Mrs Puss.

Both Bro Dog and Mrs Puss stop. Bro Dog stares at Mrs Puss with wide-open mouth, not able to say a single word.

Mrs Puss has to say, "Good morning, Bro Dog."

Still staring, Dog can't believe how well fed Mrs Puss looks. At last Dog says, "Mrs Puss, you look so well, so round, so shining! You look like a rich somebody, who hungry-time hasn't touched at all. You look like you've just landed from some foreign country."

Mrs Puss shakes her head.

"No, Bro Dog. I haven't been anywhere."

"Well, Mrs Puss, excuse me please," Dog says. "I have to ask you, where d'you have your storehouse of food hiding?"

Mrs Puss gives a little smile and says, "Bro Dog, sometimes a thief from a thief makes even the good Lord smile."

"Mrs Puss," Dog says, "can't I smile too, even a little bit? Look how I'm all skin and bone."

Mrs Puss glances at Dog with a look of pity and says, "Oh, Bro Dog, hungry-time wasted you bad-bad. You're just not the same man." Then Mrs Puss looks about her, making sure nobody else overhears her secret. "Bro Dog," she says quietly, "it can't be a bad thing to share some goodness with a good friend. I'm going to tell you something. I've found a lock-up building where meat is kept."

"Meat!" Dog blurted loudly.

"Shuuh!" Mrs Puss says. "Not so loud. I believe only a few people are getting the meat," she whispers.

"Where? Where's the meat?" Dog asks impatiently. And Dog's ears practically stand up as he listens.

Mrs Puss explains that she believes the meat is stolen. She also believes the thieves use the little building as their meat lock-up store. She has seen the men bring meat. She has also seen them come and collect meat only. The men come and go only at night. She has discovered the unusual men from her sitting in the avocado tree, beside the lock-up building, eating an avocado in darkness.

The men do everything in whispers and careful-careful movements, never to make a sound. And, the big thing is, the men don't even use a key to lock up or open up the place. They use certain magic words.

Once she realises what the men do in the darkness, she makes it her business to come back. Again and again she conceals herself in darkness and watches and listens until she learns everything perfect-perfect.

She has learnt how to open the door, close it, collect her

meat, open and close it again and go, without any trouble.

Then, seriously, Mrs Puss points out, "One thing, Bro Dog, one thing, no liver must be touched. Not one little piece of liver must be touched."

Dog gives himself a hard smile and says, "Would happen, wouldn't it? Just because any time, anywhere, I'd give anything for a piece of liver, that's the meat mustn't be touched."

"Well, Bro Dog," Mrs Puss says, "I know how much you like your piece of liver, but I've listened, I've watched, I know what will cause bad trouble."

That night, after the men come and leave again, Mrs Puss slides down from the avocado tree and calls Bro Dog to come out of hiding.

Mrs Puss and Bro Dog stand in front of the door. Mrs Puss uses the magic words, ending with "Seven, eight, nine". Slow-slow, the door opens. Mrs Puss and Bro Dog slip inside. Mrs Puss uses the magic words again, this time ending with "Nine, eight, seven". The door closes and locks them in.

They light up a tiny oil lamp.

Quick-quick and brisk, Bro Dog and Mrs Puss fill their bags with meat. All kinds of meat are seasoned, corned, pickled and packed in barrel after barrel. The meat is ready in all kinds of cuts. There is a barrel of liver and a barrel of heart. Mrs Puss doesn't show Bro Dog the liver barrel. And still Mrs Puss doesn't see when Dog's nippy movement slides the lid of the liver barrel open; he has a peep, and slides it shut again.

Bags full of meat, the oil lamp is put out.

Dog and Mrs Puss come to the door. Again Mrs Puss uses the magic words ending with "Seven, eight, nine". The door opens. Both of them slip out quickly. Mrs Puss closes the door with the magic words ending with "Nine, eight, seven".

Dog and Mrs Puss hurry away in the night with their bags of meat.

Two nights later, Mrs Puss and Bro Dog come back again. They wait in hiding. Mrs Puss is sure the men are due to arrive. But they don't come. Afraid of being caught inside, with the barrels of meat, Mrs Puss and Bro Dog wait until almost daylight. Then they decide they are not going to go home with empty bags. They'll take a chance. But they know they have to be quick.

Mrs Puss opens the door and closes it again, using the magic words.

They light up the little lamp.

Working quick-quick, listening, looking, Mrs Puss and Bro Dog load up their bags with meat already cut into pieces.

"Are you ready?" Mrs Puss whispers.

"Yes. I'm ready," Dog says.

"Right," Mrs Puss says. "I'll put out the lamp." And she blows out the light.

Thinking Bro Dog is behind her, Mrs Puss keeps whispering to him. Mrs Puss opens the door, slips out, whispering to Dog, then closes the door again. Immediately, there is panic thumping on the door inside.

Mrs Puss uses the magic words. The door doesn't open. Mrs Puss calls to Bro Dog inside, telling him to use the magic words. Mrs Puss hears the locked-in Bro Dog using the magic words properly. But the door doesn't open.

Oh! What now? That greedy Dog is trapped!

"Did you touch any liver?" Mrs Puss calls. "Have you any liver in your bag?"

"Just one – well – two little pieces," Dog says, anxious-anxious.

"Oh, Bro Dog, you're in trouble," Mrs Puss says. "And putting back the liver now won't help one bit. In any case, it's nearly daylight. I'll have to go. I'll have to go, Bro Dog. I'll get some help. I'll try and get some help."

Mrs Puss hurries away leaving Bro Dog locked up with the barrels of meat.

When Anancy hears about Bro Dog's trouble, Anancy sends Tiger a message and keeps it a secret. All the same, Mrs Puss didn't know that the meat men sometimes come and collect meat in the daytime too.

The meat men come. To the meat men's great surprise they find Bro Dog locked up with their meat.

The morning sun is high up in the sky when the three meat men tie up Bro Dog in their cart, along with their load of meat. With Dog tied up, not able to move, not able to make the slightest whimper, the men begin to take him away.

The men come out on to the country road. Sudden-sudden the meat men hear a song. They don't see him, but it's Anancy. The meat men know it's Anancy with a message in a song. They cannot ignore it. The men stop the cart to listen. Hiding himself, Anancy sings this little song:

"There's a man who's no beggar.
  Could it be the Bro Tiger?
  No-beggar Bro Tiger?
  No-beggar Bro Tiger?
  Who for liver or leg
  Just never learnt to beg
  Who for liver or leg
  Just never learnt to beg.
  He never learnt to beg, O!..."

The meat men suddenly see Tiger in the road, coming towards them. The men become panic-stricken and bundle themselves off. They run away like mad, leaving their cart.

Tiger comes up to the cart in the road. Tiger unties a very grateful Bro Dog, who takes the liver out of his bag and leaves it for Tiger.

Bro Dog picks up his bag of meat and hurries off with Anancy, who waits for him in the road.

Tiger pulls away the meat men's cart of meat for himself.

When people hear about what has happened, each person says, "Oh!" and then exclaims the proverb, "A thief from a thief makes the good Lord smile!"

ANANCY, TIGER AND THE SHINE-DANCER-SHINE

Today now, the big happening is on. Tiger and Anancy meet in a clash, in the dance against each other. You can remember how Tiger did come in on horseback at the Stump-a-Foot Celebration and spoil that first competition. Well, everybody's been waiting to see the real honest contest.

Bro Dog's hard work has done everything to fix up the event. Everywhere, pasted up posters announce:

Big Christmas Event
MATCH OF SHINE-DANCER-SHINE
between the one
BRO NANCY
and the one
BRO TIGER

Choosing Christmas-time is clever too, you see. Plenty people will come out. But specially, it's the time when Great-House will give money to dancing events in Village Square.

The time has come now. Village Square is all noisy enjoyment. Usual Christmas dancers – John-Canoo Masquerade Dancers – did just finish fantastic crowd-pleasing dances. And everybody is glad some John-Canoo Dancers stand with the crowd. And chief dancer, John-Canoo himself, sits in with the musicians, who are all dressed up in rainbow colours.

Bro Dog puts down his banjo. He steps out and speaks. "Noise makers, and stiff faces, wow wow!"

"Wow wow!" the crowd chants back.

"Wow wow!" Dog repeats.

The crowd roars back, "Wow wow!"

Dog walks round in the circle the crowd allows. And loud-loud, Dog recites:

> "Best-dancer will win.
>   Hear this, hear this, O!
> Best-dancer will have the bright-bright grin.
> Best-dancer gets Great-House prize money.
> I say, Great-House prize money.
>   Hear this, hear this, O!
> Nothing will go to what's half-dead –
> Better bring on John-Canoo Horse-Head.
> All is for dance and dancer.
>   Hear this, hear this, O!
> Bright-brightest ablaze with music-fire.
>   Hear this, hear this, O!"

The crowd goes noisy with cheering for Bro Dog. He

waits. He goes on. "Starting off this revelation of rhythm, the joy of Shine-Dancer-Shine rivalry, here is best push-you-over-easy fellow, Bro Tiger!" In the crowd-roaring Bro Dog walks back and again picks up his banjo.

And with Monkey there on drums, Rabbit on fife, Puss on fiddle, Goat on maracas and Pig rubbing grater, all the musicians strike up music, swift and hot.

Bro Tiger starts with unexpected amusement. Tiger comes out of a lying-down barrel beside the musicians. Adding to that, he's dressed up in a floppy straw hat, in too-big blue jeans trousers with braces and patchwork patches, and heavy boots not laced up.

Tiger starts his dance.

To the hot music, Tiger jigs. Tiger wiggles his hips, missing the rhythm of the music, on purpose, going round and round the circle in the middle of the crowd. Soon, it is seen that Tiger isn't all beef and no brains. Tiger has a plan.

Tiger begins to clown. Tiger begins funny mime dances, showing off that he's really a big country buffoon.

Tiger stoops. Tiger plays he's milking a cow, with all sorts of clever movements. Unexpectedly, Tiger imitates getting kicked over by the cow, swift-swift, flat onto his back. Tiger's hat falls off his head; he ignores the hat.

Tiger gets up, shakes himself off, then begins walking all droopy-droopy, all half-dead, dragging himself along, doing a lazy walk-dance, on how a lazy countryman walks. And with the crowd cheering, Tiger goes into mocking the climbing of a tree. With all lazy movements, out of beat with the music, Tiger barely manages to get one foot up against the side of the tree. It's too much hard work. He gives up. He mocks trying to get his leg back down, but even that effort is too much. Again Tiger falls flat on his back.

All this time, wild with roars, shrieks and whoopee whistles, the crowd claps with the musicians, and sings with them, this song:

> "*Poor Tatty-Tatty Pappy.*
> *Poor Pitchy-Patchy Pappy –*
> *Lost yesterday, lost tomorrow.*
> *Doesn't rent, doesn't borrow.*
> *Finds a fine-fine blackskin gal*
> *She finds a better-better pal.*
>
> *O, they cuss him and cuss-cuss him.*
> *They cuss him and they cuss him.*
> *Whai-O, they cuss-cuss him!*
> *Can't guess any riddle-mi-riddle*
> *But what a John-Canoo-man, John-Canoo-man,*
> *John-Canoo-man, John-Canoo-man,*
>   *John-Canoo-man, O!*
>   *Tatty-Tatty Pappy.*
>   *Pitchy-Patchy Pappy...*"

Tiger goes on. Tiger mocks how somebody falls about under the weight of heavy load. Tiger's mocking dance has him with one hand up holding the load. His legs are rubbery, his body wobbly. And he staggers about till his load falls on top of him, leaving him panting, half-dead.

With having the crowd noisy with enjoyment, Tiger begins to mock how a man and a woman quarrel. Doing his wiggles, Tiger stretches his neck. Tiger does snappy high-pitched yaps and grumbles. He does the man answering back, chest-beating himself, jumping up and down, with deep-voiced barks and growling.

All this time, the music with the clapping and the singing goes on:

> "...*Poor Tatty-Tatty Pappy.*
> *Poor Pitchy-Patchy Pappy—*
> *Lost yesterday, lost tomorrow.*
> *Doesn't rent, doesn't borrow.*
> *Finds a fine-fine fairskin gal*
> *She finds a better-better pal.*
>
> *O, they cuss him and cuss-cuss him.*
> *They cuss him and they cuss him.*
> *Whai-O, they cuss-cuss him!*
> *Can't guess any riddle-mi-riddle*
> *But what a John-Canoo-man, John-Canoo-man,*
> *John-Canoo-man, John-Canoo-man,*
>   *John-Canoo-man, O!*
>   *Tatty-Tatty Pappy.*
>   *Pitchy-Patchy Pappy, O!...*"

Tiger sits down, suddenly rolls onto his head, kicks up his boot-clad feet into the air tiredly, like somebody without strength to pedal a bicycle properly. Tiger gets up. One of his boots falls off. He picks it up, jigs and wiggles and waves the boot about round the circle.

The music stops. Tiger bows. The crowd cheers and cheers him till he disappears. Anancy knows Tiger has done well. Everything he does must better Tiger.

The crowd goes silent, waiting.

Then, Bro Nancy doesn't wait to be announced. Anancy comes out wearing a long gown of brown sugar bag sacking. The music and the crowd welcome Anancy big with noises. The musicians start up another song. And straightaway, Anancy-Spiderman goes into a dramatic fall-on-your-face sort of dance.

Anancy bends forward, stretches one arm down and tries to make his face look long. And, head dipping, bottom pushing sharp, an arm hanging down like a horse's front leg in movement, Anancy does a Three-Legged Ghost-Horse dance. His movements, his feet, make the three-legged sound, clop-pi-ti. Clop-pi-ti. Clop-pi-ti. Clop-pi-ti. The crowd groans, as if it thinks this is magic. Head dipping, bottom pushing sharp, arm hanging down, Anancy goes round and round the circle doing his "clop-pi-ti, clop-pi-ti" dance, to the music with clapping, and singing of this song:

> *"Number one golden-tailed monkey goes—*
> *Monkey named Molenggen-Spanneh.*
> *Monkey flies, he flies, he flies, he flies—*
> *He flies, O.*
> *Ante du du du du du—*
> *Clean gone, O!*
> *Ante du du du du du—*
> *Gone O Moleng…"*

Round and round this song is kept up, with the music and clapping. And Anancy doesn't stop.

Anancy imitates the way the Ghost-Horse looks at an audience. Anancy stops. He bends his ghostly long neck, looks at the crowd on one side and slowly dances—clop-pi-ti. Again, he bends his ghostly long neck, looking at the other side of the crowd and slowly dances—clop-pi-ti… The music is carrying on.

> *"Number one golden-tailed monkey's gone—*
> *Monkey named Molenggen-Spanneh.*
> *Monkey flies, he flies, he flies, he flies—*
> *He flies, O.*
> *Ante du du du du du—*
> *Clean gone, O!*
> *Ante du du du du du—*
> *Gone O Moleng!…"*

Dancing backwards now, like the Ghost-Horse, Anancy, head-dipping, bottom-pushing, round and round the circle, goes on with his weird clop-pi-ti, clop-pi-ti, clop-pi-ti. Clop-pi-ti, clop-pi-ti, clop-pi-ti… Then the crowd notices that the Anancy is going on with something else.

While still dancing, smart-smart, the Anancy works

himself out of his gown. The Anancy now shows off short trousers with a tight-fitting coat of glittering stars, all military looking. The tunic has red shoulder flaps. It has a red sash, like a belt over his shoulder and across his chest. The dress brings out Anancy like a grand military man. But, best of all, the dress glitters with pasted-on silver-paper stars, close together over it. This then must be the shining glory! This must be it! As the people see the Anancy's star-shining coat, their roar is unbelievable.

Didn't the posters announce "Shine-Dancer-Shine"! Bro Nancy's interpretation is all-sensational. Whistles and shrieks and roars make the people one big deafening body.

Like the Ghost-Horse taking off, Anancy wants everybody to believe he's as swift as a bird. He opens his arms wide and runs round the circle, till the music stops.

Bro Dog comes out and says, "Wow wow!"

"Wow wow!" the crowd answers back.

Wearing his masquerade mask again, with his enormous horned headdress, the John-Canoo chief dancer comes forward beside Bro Dog and shouts, "Who's for the prize?"

Everybody knows. Everybody shouts, "Shine-Dancer-Shine man, Bro Nancy!"

By this time the real Pitchy-Patchy of the John-Canoo Dancers has come back with a collection of money from the crowd, for Bro Tiger.

But Bro Nancy walks away with the most – with Great-House prize money.

From that time, all who perform for a crowd like to wear a most shining glitter-glitter costume. Anancy has a big hand in it.

ANANCY, LION AND
TIGER'S LAST DAY

This is a last meeting story – a terrible last meeting story. It's also a warning. It says, should you ever happen to hear Tiger and Lion fighting, oh, you shouldn't look. The sight is too terrible. Bro Tiger and Bro Lion have equal strength. They have it in themselves to fight to a kill, if nobody stops them.

It's such a wonder how Anancy knows when something awful is happening. And this now hits Anancy just after he has kindly offered to deliver a pan of oil – still hot – to a good neighbour. Anancy turns round swift and brisk and arrives on the scene.

Bro Tiger and Bro Lion damage each other worse and worse. They are all fight noises and eyes and weapons and blows. Their coats are ripped. Their faces and necks and bodies are cut. Lion and Tiger bleed. They smear each other all over on and on and don't care. Standing to full height, heads and arms busy, they damage each other.

"Gentlemen!" Anancy shouts. "Gentlemen, stop it!" Anancy puts down his vessel of oil. He walks round the roars and blows and blood. He raises his arms in despair and shouts, "Bro Lion, Bro Tiger, stop it, please!"

Lion and Tiger fall to the ground, locked to each other. In grips giving each other pain, they struggle onto their feet again. They stand to full height, with arms round each other's shoulders and mouths open with rage. Unexpectedly, Anancy tosses the warm oil onto their faces. Each one closes his eyes and lets go of the other.

"Enough is enough – Gentlemen!" Anancy says.

Lion and Tiger give each other one last long, terrible stare. Tiger turns slowly and walks away. Lion goes too, slowly, in the opposite direction. Both are hurt, tired and sad.

Anancy stands, thinking. He doesn't know how long Lion and Tiger have fought. He doesn't know what has started the fight. But both have their coats cut like rags. Both are dirty with smears of blood. Tiger seems to Anancy to be the sadder of the two. Unexpectedly, Anancy feels sorry for Tiger. Anancy wants to comfort Tiger. Oh, Bro Anancy wants to comfort Bro Tiger! He looks round and Tiger is gone. Anancy calls, "Bro Tiger! Bro Tiger!" No answer. And no sign of Tiger. Anancy begins to run after Tiger, where he has disappeared.

Anancy travels on all night. After sunrise Anancy sees Bro Tiger and Mrs Tiger ahead, going along. Anancy walks quicker. He catches up with Bro Tiger and Mrs Tiger and settles with walking beside them. But nobody speaks.

"Bro Tiger," Anancy says, "I'm happy you're walking well, after such a fight." Tiger walks on, taking no notice. Anancy goes on. "A giant fighter. A giant fighter you are, Bro Tiger! And only me saw it."

Nobody else speaks. On and on without speaking, Anancy and Tiger and Mrs Tiger keep on walking till late afternoon. Suddenly Anancy knows he must go back. He should go no further. He stops. Unexpectedly, Anancy hears a sound, a strange sound, as if the sea rages about like thunder in caves underground.

Anancy knows something is going to happen. He watches Tiger and Mrs Tiger going on and on alone, up a hill, never looking back, never sideways or even ahead. He watches them go over the hill and disappear onto the other side.

A sudden burst of flame splits the side of the hill where Tiger and Mrs Tiger have passed. Quick-quick, other bursts of flames open the hill into a glowing fire. The hill rolls and roars belching up burning land. Then, unexpectedly, the sea rushes in from everywhere. Bulk pieces of a broken and burning hill ride on the inrush of sea. Big glowing rocks begin to drift. Next moment the sea has swallowed every glowing spark. All is a level of sea, as if the sea has always been there.

Anancy is amazed. Then Anancy looks and sees Tiger and Mrs Tiger on level land on the other side, still going on and on.

"Goodbye, Bro Tiger!" Anancy shouts. "Goodbye!"

Brother Tiger turns and waves goodbye.

"Bro Tiger's in another land," Anancy whispers to himself.

He gets home. And Bro Nancy is surprised how much he misses Bro Tiger. Anancy decides, to keep the memory of Tiger, he'll tell stories about himself and Bro Tiger.

Spider Anancy hides in bedrooms and whispers stories like dreams. Anancy remembers more and more stories and tells them like dreams.

VAMPIRE MASTER

Virginia Ironside

There's something very sinister about Burlap Hall's new biology master, Mr A. Culard. He hates light, loves bats and eats dead flies! Now the other teachers are starting to behave oddly too. The question is: will young Tom and his friends, Susan and Miles, manage to get their teeth into the problem before it gets its teeth into them?

"A very funny novel which keeps up a steady pace of entertainment and suspense."
The Bookseller

"Entertaining...Hilarious moments."
Junior Bookshelf